Dear Reader,

You're about to experience a revolution in reading—BookShots.

BookShots are a whole new kind of book—100 percent story-driven, no fluff, always under $5.

I've written or co-written nearly all the BookShots and they're among my best novels of any length.

At 150 pages or less BookShots can be read in a night, on a commute, even on your cell phone during breaks at work.

I hope you enjoy *The All-Nighter*.

All my best,

James Patterson

P.S.

For special offers and the full list of BookShots titles, please go to **BookShots.com**

BOOK**SHOTS**

James Patterson's
BOOKSHOTS
Flames

THE WITNESSES

JAMES PATTERSON
BRENDAN DUBOIS

BOOKSHOTS

Little, Brown and Company

New York Boston London

Copyright © 2017 JBP Business, LLC

Hachette Book Group supports the right to free expression and the value of copyright. The purpose of copyright is to encourage writers and artists to produce the creative works that enrich our culture.

The scanning, uploading, and distribution of this book without permission is a theft of the author's intellectual property. If you would like permission to use material from the book (other than for review purposes), please contact permissions@hbgusa.com. Thank you for your support of the author's rights.

BookShots / Little, Brown and Company
Hachette Book Group
1290 Avenue of the Americas, New York, NY 10104
bookshots.com

Originally published as an ebook, July 2016
First paperback edition, December 2017

BookShots is an imprint of Little, Brown and Company, a division of Hachette Book Group, Inc. The Little, Brown name and logo are trademarks of Hachette Book Group, Inc. The BookShots name and logo are trademarks of JBP Business, LLC.

The publisher is not responsible for websites (or their content) that are not owned by the publisher.

The Hachette Speakers Bureau provides a wide range of authors for speaking events. To find out more, go to hachettespeakersbureau.com or call (866) 376-6591.

ISBN 978-0-316-41874-4

THE WITNESSES

CHAPTER 1

IN A PERFECT world, Ronald Temple wouldn't be sitting in his Barcalounger in the living room of his retirement home in Levittown, New York, with the side window open and a blanket across his legs, wishing a rifle was in his lap, ready to kill the terrorists living next door.

Yeah, he thinks, lowering his Zeiss 7x50 binoculars. In a perfect world, the Twin Towers would still be standing, scores of his friends would still be alive, and he wouldn't be slowly dying here in suburbia, lungs clogged with whatever crap he breathed in while working the pile for weeks after 9/11.

The light-blue house next door is normal, like the rest of the homes in his neighborhood, built in 1947 in an old potato field on Long Island. It was the beginning of the postwar rush to suburbia. Levittown is now a great place to go to school, raise families, or retire, like Ronald and his wife, Helen, are doing.

But their new neighbors?

Definitely not normal.

Ronald lifts up the binoculars again.

They had moved in just three days ago, when it was overcast, the dark-gray clouds threatening rain. A black GMC Yukon had pulled into the narrow driveway and a family had tumbled out, all dark-skinned, all in Western clothes they looked uncomfortable wearing. An adult male and an adult female—apparently the parents—and a boy and a girl. Ronald had been sitting in this same chair, his oxygen machine gently wheezing, tubes rubbing up against his raw nostrils, as he saw them hustle into the house.

And the woman and the young girl both had head coverings on.

It was a bit suspicious at first, so Ronald had watched the activities next door as much as possible, and he became more concerned with every passing minute and hour. No moving van had pulled in after that first day. Only a few suitcases and duffel bags had been brought into the house—quickly, from the Yukon. And the adults had not come over to introduce themselves to either him or his wife.

He moves the binoculars in a slow, scanning motion.

There.

He sees a large man walk past the kitchen window across the way.

That was the other thing that had gotten his attention three days ago.

Their driver.

Oh, yeah, their driver.

He had emerged first from the Yukon and Ronald could tell he was a professional: he wore a jacket to hide whatever hardware he was carrying, his eyes swept the yard and driveway, looking for threats, and he had kept his charges inside the Yukon while he had first gone into the house to check everything out.

Like the other four, he was dark-skinned. He was nearly bald. Although he wasn't too muscular—not an NFL lineman on steroids—he was bulky enough, similar to those Emergency Service Unit guys Ronald had met during his time in the NYPD.

A bodyguard, then?

Or maybe the terrorist cell leader?

Ronald sweeps the house again, back and forth, back and forth. He keeps up on newspapers, television, and internet news and knows this is the new way of terrorism and violence. People nowadays move into a quiet neighborhood, blend in, and then go out and strike.

The kids?

Camouflage.

The husband and wife?

Like that couple that had shot up that holiday party in San Bernardino, California, last year.

They blended in.

And the bulky guy…maybe he was their trainer, or maybe their leader?

He was probably ready to prime them to go out and kill.

Ronald lowers his binoculars, adjusts the oxygen hose around his head again. It was just too damn strange, too damn out of the ordinary. No moving vans, no friends stopping by; neither the husband nor the wife—if they were really married, who knew— left to go to work in the morning. No deliveries, no lawn mowing, nothing.

They are definitely hiding out.

Ronald wishes once more for the comfortable weight of an AR15 across his lap. To take down a cell like this one requires firepower, and lots of it. With a 20-round magazine and open iron sights—he sure as hell didn't need a telescopic sight at this range—he could take care of the three adults with no problem. If, for example, he saw them walking out to the Yukon, wearing coats, trying to hide weapons or a suicide bomber's belt, he could knock them all down with an AR15 before they even got into their SUV.

A series of cramps run up his thin legs, making him grimace with pain. And the kids? Leave 'em be…unless they picked up a weapon and decided to come over here and get revenge. Lots of kids that age were doing the same thing overseas, tossing grenades, grabbing AK-47s, setting up IEDs.

He picks up the binoculars once more.

In his twenty-one years on the New York police force, Ronald drew his service weapon only three times—twice at traffic stops and once while checking out a bodega robbery—but he knows that if he had to, he'd do what it took to get the job done, even today, as crippled as he is.

He removes one hand from the binoculars, checks the lumpy shape under his blanket, resting on his lap. It's his backup weapon from when he was on the job, a .38 Smith & Wesson Police Special.

Ronald nods with satisfaction. He'd had a chance once to be a hero on 9/11, and he blew it.

He's not going to let another chance slip by.

CHAPTER 2

LANCE SANDERSON WALKS into the kitchen of the rental home to get another cup of coffee. His wife, Teresa, is working at her laptop set on the round wooden dining table, and he gives her neck a quick rub as he goes by. Teresa has a nest of notebooks and papers and other reference books nearby as she types slowly and deliberately.

After pouring himself a cup, Lance asks, "Get you a refill?"

"Not right now, hon," she says. "Maybe later."

He stands at her side, takes a sip. Due to the last few weeks out in the harsh North African sun, his wife's skin has darkened, making her look even more radiant than usual. The sun had streaked her light brown hair, wavy and shoulder length, and had bronzed her legs and arms. Even after two kids, she's kept her body in good shape, with long legs and a cute round bottom. He remembers with pleasure the first time they made love, when both were in grad school. She had whispered, "My boobs aren't much, but they're designed for babies. The rest of me is yours...and wants a real man."

Lance rubs her neck again and she sighs softly, like a satisfied cat. "What's new?" he asks.

She doesn't look up from her keyboard as she continues writing. "The old perv next door is still staring over here with his binoculars."

"I told you to stop flashing him your butt," Lance says. "What do you expect?"

"Har-de-hah-hah," she says, which cheers up Lance. Nice to see her in a good mood after the past week. "If I did that, all he'd see is the desert sand I'm still picking out of my butt crack." She lifts her head from the keyboard and gives the kitchen a glance. "I miss home," she says. "I miss the ocean. I miss the fruit trees. I miss our backyard."

"Me, too."

She nods at the avocado-colored refrigerator and the bright-yellow kitchen countertop. "Just look at this dump. It looks like it was redecorated when we had a peanut farmer for president."

"Or a movie actor," he says. "How goes the guidebook?"

"Oh, that," she says, running a hand across her notes and the piles of books scattered across the table. "In these times, m'dear, it sure is hard to do research without having internet access."

Lance sips again from his coffee. "I know. Trying to do the same, cataloguing Carthaginian potsherds without knowing if you're repeating yourself or the work of others."

Then Lance feels a sudden chill, like a window has been opened in the house, or an unexpected eclipse has blocked out the sun.

Close enough.

The man they know as Jason Tyler is in their kitchen. Lance tries not to step back in fear. At first glance, Jason isn't too large or hulking, but that's just the first glance. In the few days he and his family have gotten to know him, Lance has learned that Jason likes to wear comfortable sneakers, loose slacks, and short-sleeve shirts, like the ones he's wearing today: gray slacks and black shirt, shirttails hanging over his slim waist. It took Teresa one night in a hotel room in Marseilles to point out the obvious: "Honey, he dresses like that to hide his muscles and whatever weapons he's carrying."

The man is six feet, with broad shoulders and a head that is covered with just the bare stubble of black hair. His skin is dark, and it's funny, but if Jason turns one way in the light, he looks vaguely Asian, but from another angle, he can also look like he's from the Middle East.

A chameleon, Lance thinks, *a chameleon who is tougher than steel.*

Jason says, "You two all right in here?"

Lance says, "Doing okay."

Jason's eyes never stop. They're always moving, looking, evaluating. He nods just a bit. "I know you like to work here in the kitchen, ma'am, but I wish you would find another spot. That window makes you vulnerable."

"I like the light," Teresa says.

"It makes you vulnerable."

Lance sees his wife's hands tighten. "Are you ordering me?"

A slight pause. "No." Another pause. "I've checked in on Sandy. And Sam. Both seem to be doing well. I'm going out on the grounds for a few minutes. You know the drill."

Lance sighs. "Yes. Stay indoors. At all times."

And Jason leaves. Just like that. A big man, with those hidden muscles…Lance thinks he would move like an ox or a bull, trampling and bumping into things. But this man…he moves like a dark-colored jaguar, on the prowl, always hunting.

The kitchen's temperature seems to warm up about five degrees.

Teresa goes back to the keyboard, types two or three words, stops. Looks up at her husband.

"Lance."

"Right here."

"Do you trust what he says?" Teresa asks.

"About what?"

"That if we were to use the internet, we could be dead by the end of the day?"

He reaches out, rubs the back of her neck, and it's tense. No sweet sighs this time. "We have to trust him. We have to."

Lance feels out of time, out of place. How in the world did his family end up here?

"We're in too deep," Lance says. "We have no choice."

Teresa turns so she's looking directly at him. His hand falls away. Her pretty dark-brown eyes tear up.

"But what about our kids?" she asks. "What choice do they have?"

From the other side of the house, a boy's voice cries out. "Dad! I need you! Right now!"

His own eyes watering, Lance rushes out of the kitchen without saying a word.

CHAPTER 3

RONALD TEMPLE IS startled by the noise and realizes he has drifted off. His hand automatically goes under the blanket to his .38 Smith & Wesson revolver as Helen comes in. He relaxes his hand when he sees his wife, thinks how close he came to doing something stupid. In his years on the job, he knew of at least two instances where fellow patrolmen were accidentally shot by their partners in a moment of panic or fear, and it feels good to bring his empty hand up.

In those two cases on the job, the shootings had been successfully covered up, but Ronald doubts he could get away with making up a story about some random ganghanger shooting his wife in their living room.

Helen manages to smile at him as she comes over. It's not that warm a day, but she's wearing a knee-length simple floral dress with a thin black belt around her thickening waist. Decades into their marriage there are wrinkles and more bulges than usual, and her black hair is secretly colored, but he knows he's lucked out with her, a now retired schoolteacher who most times has the knack of calming him down.

She kisses the top of his head and pats his thin shoulder. "How's the spying going?" she asks.

He resists snapping back at her, not wanting to hear what might come out of her mouth, even though she's got a cheery expression on her face. Helen is almost always cheerful, but she keeps a tight lid on her resentments and frustrations. He recalled with regret getting into a fight with her some years ago, after mention was made of their two sons, Tucker and Spencer. One worked as cop in the LAPD and the other was an Oregon State Trooper. Helen had said, "Of course our boys moved west. Do you think they wanted to listen to you bitch at them about how they're doing their jobs wrong, and how you would do it better?"

So Ronald smiles and says, "Just keeping watch, that's all. If more people kept watch, this would be a safer country."

Helen keeps a slim hand on his shoulder, rubs him for a few seconds. "You're right, but... really, Ronald. You really think that family next door means trouble?"

Ronald takes a breath, tries not to cough with all that 9/11 crap in his lungs. He had been a security officer for an investment firm in the South Tower. Although he had been home sick on 9/11, he had spent weeks there later, working and doing penance.

"Look. They're not from around here. They keep to themselves. And I don't like that big guy walking around, like he's their private security or something. It just doesn't make sense."

His wife looks out to the house and he's irritated again—as a civilian, she can't see what he sees. All she sees is a simple house with simple people living inside. She can't see beyond that.

Helen says, "Really? You think terrorists are going to hide out here, in Levittown? And besides... they've got kids."

"Terrorists have used kids as a cover before," Ronald says impatiently. "And why not Levittown? It's got history, the first true suburbia in the country, it's as pure America as it gets. A perfect hideout, a perfect target. You know how terrorists like to hit at targets that make a lot of news. Why not here?"

His wife turns around, heads to the kitchen. "Then call the cops already, Ronald. If you feel that strongly about it, don't just sit here and fume. Do something about it."

Ronald feels the weight of the revolver in his lap. He is doing something about it, he thinks, and aloud he says, "The cops are too PC now. They won't do anything. Hell, they might even charge me with a hate crime or something."

Helen doesn't say anything in reply and he wonders if she didn't hear him, or is ignoring him. What the hell—what difference did it make?

Ronald picks up the binoculars, looks over at the house again. The man is talking to the woman, who appears to be working on a laptop.

But where's the big guy? The muscle? The cell leader?

He carefully scans the windows, the kitchen, the master bedroom, and the living room.

Nothing.

Where the hell is he?

No attached garage, and since he knows the house is practically identical to his own, there's no basement or attic, so—

A knock on the door.

He's seized with fear. "Don't answer it!"

But again, Helen either isn't listening or is ignoring him. She goes to the door and opens it up, and Ronald drops the binoculars in his blanket-covered lap.

It's the threatening guy from next door.

He stares at his wife.

Helen steps back.

He says one sentence, full of menace:

"You need to stop."

CHAPTER 4

LANCE MOVES QUICKLY through the house, again hearing Sam's plaintive yell—"Dad!"—and a moment later steps into his son's room. They've been here only a few days and already the ten-year-old boy's room is a cluttered mess. The bed is unmade, the temporary bookshelves are cluttered with rocks and books, and clothing is scattered across the floor like a whirlwind has just struck. Posters of San Francisco Giants players are taped up on the yellow walls.

Sam's face is red and he's sitting in an old school chair, in front of a small desk that's scattered with tiny white plastic bones. A cardboard box with a brightly colored image of a dinosaur—a *T. rex*?—is on the floor. He's wearing blue jeans, a black T-shirt, and white scuffed sneakers.

"What's up, sport?" Lance asks, going straight to his boy.

Sam jerks his chin to the left. "It's Sandy. She just came in here and took my book about triceratops. Without even asking!"

Lance rubs the boy's light brown hair. Sam looks a lot like his mother. "Okay. Anything else?"

"Yeah, can you get it back? And when are we leaving here? I'm bored."

"I'm bored, too. Let me go get your book."

Lance steps out and goes into the small bedroom next door, and what a difference. The bed is made. The small, open closet shows shoes lined up and clothes hung properly. There is a small desk with a chair—identical to Sam's—but there's nothing on it. Homemade bookcases line the far wall as well, but they are filled with rows of books, all placed in alphabetical order by author. Sandy, two years older than her brother, is on her bed reading a book, her back and shoulders supported by two pillows.

The book has a dinosaur on the cover. Lance steps forward. "Sandy? Hon?"

She ignores him, flipping a page, reading some more. Her blond hair—lightened by the North African sun—has been styled into two braids.

"Sandy?"

"Let me finish this paragraph, please."

Lance waits. Then she looks up, face inquisitive, light-blue eyes bright and intelligent.

"Yes?"

Lance says, "Is that Sam's book?"

"Yes."

"He says you took it without permission."

"I didn't need permission," she says crisply. "The book wasn't being used. It was on the shelf. Sam is working on a dinosaur model. It has 102 parts. He can't work on a dinosaur model with that many parts and read this book at the same time."

"Still, you should have asked permission."

"But I needed the book."

"Why do you need the book?" Lance asks.

"Because I've read all of my books," she explains. "I needed something new to read, and if I were to ask my brother for permission, he might have said no, and then I would still have nothing to read. So I did the right thing and took the book to my room."

Perfectly logical, Lance thinks, *and perfectly Sandy.*

"But it's his book."

"He wasn't using it. I needed something to read."

Lance holds out his hand. "Give me the book, Sandy. You can borrow one of mine."

Her eyes widen with anticipation. "Really? Which one?"

"*Hannibal and His Times,*" Lance says.

His twelve-year-old daughter frowns. "By Lewis Chapman?"

"Yes."

"Dad, I read that last September. I read it from September 17th to September 19th."

Lance smiles. "That was the hardcover edition. The paperback edition is out, with a new afterword and a rewrite of several of the chapters. You could read it and compare and contrast."

Sandy seems to ponder that for a moment, nods, and gives the book on triceratops back to him. "Deal. How long before you can get me that book, Dad?"

"In about ten minutes, I suppose."

She checks her watch. "It's 2:05 p.m. I'll expect you back by 2:15."

Lance says, "Of course, hon."

*   *   *

Back in Sam's room, Lance gives his son his book back, and Sam smiles and says, "Thanks, Dad." He takes the book and tosses it up on the near bookshelf and misses. It falls to the floor.

"Dad?"

"Yes, Sam?"

Sam returns to his toy dinosaur bones. "Dad, don't forget your promise, about taking us to the Badlands later this summer. I want to help out on a dinosaur dig. You said you'd check with Professor Chang at school. You promised."

"I sure did," Lance says, recalling that promise, made back when things were so much simpler and safer. "And we'll see about that, okay?"

Sam's head is still bowed over the cluttered table. "See about what?"

Lance quickly turns away from his boy, unable to speak, his throat thick, his eyes watering, thinking only one thing:

We'll see if we're all still alive by the end of this week, never mind this summer.

CHAPTER 5

RONALD'S HAND SLIPS clumsily under his blanket, grabbing the .38 revolver. Helen backs into the house, followed by the big guy from next door. *Damn it!* If he were the man he once was, he would have answered the door and gone face-to-face with this clown, and he would be standing in front of his wife, protecting her.

He slips off the oxygen tubes from his nose and heaves himself off the chair. Wrapping the blanket around himself and the hidden revolver, he strains to walk as fast as he can to his wife. "What the hell is going on here?" he shouts, hating how weak and hoarse his voice sounds. Being a cop and then a security officer means having a voice of command, and that command voice is gone.

The large man from next door has a voice that is strong and forceful. He says, "I apologize for bothering you, but I'm hoping you'll stop."

He's not too tall or too wide, and his dark clothes are loose, but Ronald senses his power and ability. He knows that man would be able to meet any challenge, whether it's intimidating a neighbor or a street gang.

"Stop what?" Ronald asks, standing next to Helen, holding the blanket around himself with one hand, his other hand hidden underneath, grasping the revolver. The damn thing feels as heavy as if it's made of lead. He feels guilty, on the spot, like a young boy called to the front of the class by the teacher.

His observing, his viewing, his…spying. Had he been noticed? Was this bulky guy going to threaten him and Helen?

The man smiles, but it doesn't comfort Ronald. The smile just shows perfect white teeth—no humor, no friendship. "If you could please stop parking your car on the street so close to our driveway," he says. "It makes it challenging to back out of our driveway without scraping our fender."

Helen clasps her hands together, steps forward, going into peacekeeper mode—like when they were raising their two hellion boys—and she says, "Absolutely. I'll go out in a few minutes and move it. Sorry to be a bother."

The smile widens, which makes the man look even fiercer. "No bother at all." And he shifts his gaze, looks straight over at Ronald. "You be careful, too, all right?"

The man turns and slips out. After Helen shuts the door, Ronald says, "Why did you say yes so quick? I wanted to ask him who he is, what he's doing here, how long they plan to stay. Damn it."

He struggles to turn around without tripping over the blanket and goes back to his chair, where he settles back down, puts the oxygen tube back under his nose, and takes a deep breath through his nostrils. He tries not to let the tickling in his lungs explode into a full-scale coughing fit.

Helen comes over, hands still clasped, face nervous. "I just wanted him out of the house. Can you blame me?"

Ronald looks out the window. The big guy is at the house, going into the front door, but, damn, look at how his head moves. He's always scanning, always looking, always evaluating.

"Did you hear him?" Ronald asks, turning back to Helen. "'Be careful, too,' he said. Like he knows I've been watching. Like he knows I'm carrying. That guy…he's smart. And tough."

Helen stands by him, looks over the tidy grass and to the house. *My God,* Ronald thinks, *for years they had seen tenants go in and out of that house, and, except for a couple of phone calls about noise complaints, it had been a peaceful place.*

Now? That simple little house seems as dangerous as a crack den.

Or worse.

Ronald asks, "Did you see his eyes? Did you?"

"What about his eyes?" Helen asks.

Ronald settles back into his chair, breathes deeply through his nostrils, and shifts the revolver around so it's easily accessible. Memories come back to him, some of them dark indeed.

"Back when I was on the job, even before 9/11, we'd get security alerts, and we'd be shown mugshots of various terrorists and shooters who could be a threat, who could be in the city."

The tickling in his lungs suddenly gets worse, and he coughs and coughs and coughs. Helen goes to a nearby little table, removes some tissues, and wipes his chin and lips, and he coughs some more.

Ronald finally catches his breath, but he can't stop wheezing. "All the mugshots of those men, they were white, black, brown, every skin color under the sun. But they all had one thing in common: the stone-cold look of a killer in their eyes."

He coughs one more time. "Just like him."

CHAPTER 6

MORE THAN 3,600 miles from the suburb of Levittown, Gray Evans is sitting at an outdoor café in Paris, his long, muscular legs stretched out. Sipping another glass of *vin ordinaire,* he watches the world in this part of the City of Lights go by.

This arrondissement isn't the neighborhood near the Eiffel Tower, of green parks and the Quai d'Orsay, of pricey restaurants and American tourists strolling around on well-lit streets, of bateaux sliding along the Seine, carrying long rows of sightseers. Nope, this part of Paris is on the outskirts, with narrow streets, even narrower alleyways always stinking of urine, and angry-looking men walking in groups of five or six. At this time of night, not a woman is to be found here.

Based on how dumpy the little café looked, Gray had half-expected to be served *la viande de cheval.* Still, the place served a nice steak frites. And the wine was cheap and filling.

As he watches the people scurrying by on the narrow street, punctuated by the burping sound of a Vespa scooter, he spots his contact. A swarthy-looking young man with thick black curly hair, wearing baggy jeans and a tan sport jacket. Gray sips again from the wineglass, checks his watch, and decides to amuse himself by watching how long it will take for his contact to meet him.

The young man walks up and down the far sidewalk, studiously ignoring Gray, and then makes a point of looking into a shop window, like he's seeing if he's being followed. Even the worst agent in France's counterterrorist unit—*Direction générale de la sécurité intérieure,* or DCRI for short—would have spotted this clown minutes ago, even if said DCRI agent was blind in one eye and confined to a wheelchair.

Gray checks his watch. Nearly ten minutes have passed and he's about to go across the road and grab the kid by the scruff of his neck to drag him over to his table, but then the young man makes his move.

He trots across the street like both ankles are sprained, and sinks into a chair across the small round table.

"Bon soir," he says, whispering, voice hoarse.

Gray nods. The young man smells of sweat and cooked onions. Gray reaches into a coat pocket, slips out the torn half of a ten-euro note, the one with a Romanesque arch on one side and a bridge on the other, and slides it across the table, past the plates and silverware.

The man has half of a ten-euro note as well, and his piece matches Gray's perfectly. He grins, like he's proud he's done so well undercover.

"My name is Yussuf," he says.

"Nice to meet you," Gray lies. "Would you like something to eat? Or drink?"

A quick shake of the head. "No. I have no time."

Gray smiles. "You're in one of the finest cities in the West, with food and drink envied around the world, and don't have the time?"

Yussuf shakes his head again and keeps on looking around the street and café, like he's expecting the entire force of the Paris Police Prefecture to rappel down these concrete and brick walls nearby and jump on his empty head.

"We have a job for you," he whispers.

"I'm sure you do," Gray says. "What is it?"

A hand goes back under Yussuf's stained coat and comes out with a slip of paper and a color photograph. Both are passed over and Gray looks down, without touching either the paper or the photograph.

Yussuf says, "We need for you to go to America and kill a target. In a place in the New York State. Called Levittown."

Gray memorizes the four faces in the color photograph.

"Why?" he asks.

The young man seems taken aback. "I thought…an understanding had been reached earlier."

Gray shrugs. "The agreement has been reached, yes. But I don't go in blind, ever. I need to know the why."

Yussuf reaches over the cluttered table and taps a face on the photo. "The target, here, it stole something from us."

"Don't you want it back?"

Yussuf draws his hand back. "It's gone beyond that…a decision has been made, and a lesson needs to be taught."

Gray says, "All right, I can understand that. Anything else?"

"The target…when you get there, may be with its family," Yussuf says. "You should take that into account."

Gray looks down at the photo again, of the four smiling faces—dad, mom, daughter, and son. "Do you want me to kill them all?"

Yussuf leans forward, lowers his voice even more. "Is that a problem?"

Two scooters race by on the narrow road, horns blaring, young men sitting on the little machines yelling at each other. When it's quiet, it's Gray's turn to lean forward.

"No," he says quietly. "Not a problem."

CHAPTER 7

JASON TYLER HAS gone to more than half the continents of the world in service to his nation. He's jumped out of planes, swum rivers, has fired weapons and has been fired upon, and has negotiated and dealt with people from Afghan tribesmen to the elite members of the British Special Air Service. But none of it has prepared him for dealing with this angry young American mother.

"Look," Teresa Sanderson says, arms crossed, standing in the kitchen, "I just want to go for a walk in the neighborhood, all right? Clear my head, stretch my limbs, get a bit of fresh air before going to bed."

Jason says, "I'm sorry, ma'am. I can't allow that. You know the rules. All of you must stay in my presence at all times. The only way you're leaving this house is if your family joins you. And at this time of the night, nobody's leaving."

Teresa walks to the kitchen door, puts her hand on the handle, like she's daring him. "And what are you going to do if I open this door and walk out?"

"I'm going to do my job," he says, glancing away for just a moment. "My job...to defend all of you, to the maximum extent."

Teresa stares at Jason, and he stares back, and she says, "I'm sorry. I can't stand this anymore." She storms out of the kitchen and Jason hears the door to her and her husband's bedroom slam shut. Voices are raised. He shakes his head and goes down the hallway, heading to the kids' rooms.

A knock on the first door, and the little girl says, "You may enter."

He opens the door and takes one step into the clean and tidy room. He says, "You all right, Sandy?"

The young girl is in bed, blankets pulled up to her chest, a thick book in her slender hands. "I'm fine," she says, not lifting her gaze from the book. "Why shouldn't I be fine?"

"Ah…" Jason has spent a number of days alongside this pretty young girl and still can't figure her out. "Okay, just checking."

As he leaves, she says, "Oh, Mister Tyler?"

"Yes, hon?"

"What's your birthday?"

"Ah…May thirtieth."

"And the year?"

He tells her the year. Young Sandy nods her head with satisfaction.

"You were born on a Monday," she says.

He's amazed. "That's right," he says.

She returns to her book. "Of course I'm right. I'm never wrong."

The young boy's mess of a room brings back fond memories of Jason's own, when he gave his single mom such a hard time growing up in Seattle. The boy looks up eagerly and says, "Yeah, I'm fine. Look, can I ask you something?"

"Sure."

"Are you a soldier?"

Jason isn't about to go into the details of being in the armed forces before working for one of the many intelligence services operating out there in the shadows, so he says, "Yeah, I am."

"You ever fire a gun?"

"Lots of times."

"Can I see your gun?"

Jason smiles. "Good night, kid."

Outside, the night air is warm and comfortable. Jason walks around the perimeter of the house, checking the windows, checking the doors. Sweet kids, sweet family. He hopes they will all be asleep in a while, because that will make his job easier. He doesn't need a full night's sleep—not for a while, and not for the duration of this op—but he will be happy when this job is done. He has survived and done well in circumstances that were much worse, in places that even the smartest American couldn't find on a map.

Jason looks next door, where the old man and woman live. Nosy neighbors. He hopes they won't be a problem.

He pauses at the rear, near the bedroom windows. More voices from the master bedroom.

Still, one big thing is bothering him, one very big thing.

He hates lying to that nice lady, even if she is pissed at him.

Because his classified orders are clear, quite clear.

If things go bad, and go bad quickly, he will have to do something that will make him hate himself for the rest of his life.

There's a crackling noise in the far shrubbery, bordering another home. His hands move on their own, one taking out a 9mm Beretta pistol and the other a monocular night vision scope. He starts scanning the rear yard, and there's something moving, and it's—

—a fat raccoon, waddling its way through a supposedly safe neighborhood in this supposedly safe country.

Jason lowers his weapon and his night vision scope, looks around at the calm and pleasant lights of suburbia.

"Christ," he says. "I wish I was back in Kabul."

CHAPTER 8

LANCE SANDERSON IS hanging up his shirt and pants when his wife barrels into the bedroom. Without a word, she goes to the closet, pulls out a black duffel bag, and starts throwing clothes inside.

"Honey, what's going on?"

Teresa says nothing. She tugs clothes out of the closet so hard that the empty wire hangers clang into each other.

"Teresa…" He feels foolish standing there in the bedroom, just wearing his boxer shorts. But knowing his wife, he can't ignore what's going on.

"I'm tired of being on the run," she says, bringing the duffel bag over to the bed and dropping it down with a heavy *thump*. "I'm so damn tired of it. We're eating crappy food, we're scared all the time…hell, we don't even have the right clothes! Remember the first day we got here, it was about to rain, and I had to put scarves on Sandy and me? I can't stand it."

Lance takes a breath, steps forward. "But what can we do? What choice do we have?"

Teresa looks at him, her eyes sharp. "We have a choice right now. We leave. We be careful, keep a low profile, hook up with my cousin Leonard…"

"Your cousin Leonard would be out of his league," Lance says. "He's a good cop, a brave guy, but—"

Teresa interrupts him. "Maybe, but he's family. I can trust family. I don't know if I can trust…them."

"But…we have something important, or so they say," Lance says, wondering if he can possibly defuse this situation before the kids hear them. "We need to wait here before we pass on what we've got to the right people. And we can't do that if we're on the run on our own, keeping our heads down."

Teresa stops on her way back to the closet. "You believed them? Really? Look, you can tell me now, Lance…what really went on at the dig? What nearly killed us over there?"

"You know what happened," he says. "You were there."

"Not all of the time," she says. "I find it hard to believe their bullshit story about what we supposedly have…and you swallowed it, hook, line and proverbial sinker. Tell me what really went on. There was a dispute over the pay at the dig site, wasn't there? You pissed off the wrong people, right?"

Despising himself, Lance feels anger starting to build. "Every season, there's always a dispute about pay. It's nothing new. I've told you a million times: there's nothing to tell. You were there. And what went on…it had nothing to do with money."

Their eyes are locked on each other, and she goes back to the closet. "Fine…so says you. You want to keep secrets like them? Go right ahead. After all, you've already given up your responsibility."

Lance asks, "What responsibility?"

"To be a man," Teresa snaps. "A husband. A father. To protect this family…and not to outsource it, like one of your diggers at a site."

Lance opens his mouth but finds there's nothing he can say. Her words are to the point, hurtful, and, worst of all, they're the truth. He knows what he is, an academic more at home at a dig site than in a conflict or a confrontation, and now he's let his family get bossed around and moved halfway across the world, like the weakling he is.

Teresa runs a hand across her face, and her eyes fill with tears. "Sorry, hon, that was a cheap shot. You don't deserve it."

Lance steps forward, eases her into a hug, and feels a rush of gratitude when she hugs him back hard. She whispers, "I'm so scared. I'm sorry…but I'm so scared. No matter what happened over there…I'm scared now."

He rubs her lower back. "We'll get out of this. I promise. We'll be safe."

Lance stands there for a minute, just holding his wife tight, and there's a slight knock on the door. Teresa kisses his neck and he gently breaks away, throws on a light-blue terrycloth robe, goes to answer the door.

Jason is there. "I'm going lights-out in a few minutes. Everything okay?"

Lance looks to Teresa. She bites her lower lip and gives a slight nod. He turns back to Jason and says, "Everything's fine."

Jason nods and turns away. Lance closes the bedroom door and goes to the bed, takes the duffel bag off, and puts it on the floor.

Teresa says, "Did you see it?"

Lance has no idea what she means by her question, so he decides just to go along and plead ignorance. "I'm sorry, see what?"

"That man's face," Teresa says. "There's something going on. He looks…"

"Guilty," Lance says, finishing her phrase. "Yeah, he looks guilty. I've seen it, too. Like…he's keeping some secret from us."

"But what?"

Lance says, "Honey, I don't know. I just don't know."

CHAPTER 9

AT THE LITTLE streetside café in Paris, Gray Evans checks his watch. Time to wrap up this little meet and greet.

He asks Yussuf, "Did you support the team that came in here two Novembers ago?"

The other man grins. "No, but I knew most of them...and respected them for what they did. Brave martyrs, they were."

Gray nods as if in sympathy, but in reality he thinks, *No, they were stupid fools.* It's one thing to strike at your enemies, but to get yourself killed in the process? What's the point? Gray knows he could never convince this man before him, a true believer.

Yussuf says, "So, it is agreed then?"

"Yes," Gray says.

The young man brings out a handheld device. "I shall arrange your payment." His dirty fingers manipulate the screen and he says, "It is done."

Gray has his own iPhone in his hands, sees a healthy deposit has just been made in his Cayman Islands numbered account. "All right," he says. "We have a deal."

He puts the phone away and picks up a white napkin, starts

absentmindedly rubbing the handles of his knife and fork. Yussuf ignores his movements and says, "Two things more, if I may."

"Go ahead," Gray says, feeling a soothing sensation come over him as he works on the silverware.

"You are an American. Why do you do this? In your country? To your own tribe?"

Gray finishes off his *vin ordinaire,* starts rubbing the glass as well with the cloth napkin. A small battered Renault taxi rolls by, its exhaust choking him for a moment.

"To be an American once meant something," Gray says softly. "You were part of a people and country that was respected and feared. When an American walked the street or a fighter plane took to the air, or a ship to sea, the world took notice. The world now mocks us, teases us. We've given up. We concern ourselves with silly things, like the style of a candidate's hair or which bathroom people should use. That's the way of losers. I don't associate with losers."

Yussuf says, "I see what you mean. And here is the other thing."

From his coat, he pulls out a small envelope. "I was told to give this to you and have you read it before I depart."

Gray opens the small envelope, reads the slip of paper contained within. He looks up at Yussuf and says, "Do you know what was in here?"

"No."

"Good."

With the cloth napkin, he picks up the sharp steak knife he had earlier used, quickly leans over the table, grabs Yussuf's hair with his free left hand, and shoves the knife into his right eye. Yussuf coughs, shudders, and collapses. Gray slips the knife out, gently pushes the body back so it's slumped against the chair, like Yussuf has eaten or drunk too much.

Gray gets up, retrieves Yussuf's phone, the family photo, the piece of paper with the word "Levittown" scribbled upon it, and the envelope with the small sheet of paper. He rereads its bold-faced writing and smiles to himself.

KILL YUSSUF FOR A BONUS.

CHAPTER 10

IN A CUBE-SHAPED glass-and-metal building in an obscure office park outside of Arlington, Virginia, an intelligence officer known by most as "the Big Man" looks up as his office door opens. A woman strides in without announcing herself and without having knocked. She's rail-thin, wearing a red dress and a white leather belt, and her blond hair is cut short and to the point. Her thin arms are weighted down by gold bangles and she says, "We have a problem with the Sanderson family."

The Big Man nods. "Go on."

The woman—known to most as "the Thin Woman"—says, "We got a text this a.m. from their minder. The family's getting restless, making threats to leave on their own. You know we can't let that happen."

"I know," the Big Man says. "But that's the choice they demanded in exchange for their cooperation. Low-key, not staying at a military base, keep it simple for their children's sake."

The Thin Woman says, "We could have a response team in place in their neighborhood."

He says, "That just adds another level of complexity. A unit like that can't be hidden, you have to notify local law enforcement, rumors and tales get spread around…no, they stay in place. Besides, we have more to worry about than just that."

"What is it?" she asks.

He opens up a red-bordered manila folder and says, "Our brothers and sisters at the NSA say they're picking up chatter about the Sanderson family from cells located in North Africa. No decrypt yet, but you can be sure they're not discussing sending the family a fruit basket. A hit squad is being dispatched to find them."

"Damn," the Thin Woman says. "Can we move the Sandersons?"

"Moving makes them more vulnerable."

She asks, "How much longer?"

"Two days, I hope," the Big Man says. "We need Clarkson to debrief them, and she's currently stuck at the Libyan/Egyptian border near Salloum. She's getting extracted as soon as we can make it happen."

"Why Clarkson?"

The Big Man grows irritated. His day has just started and already it's in the crapper. "You saw my memo. She's the only one with the necessary talents to do the debrief. So we have to wait until she gets stateside."

The Thin Woman shakes her head, goes to the door. "You're gambling with their lives."

The Big Man sighs. "That's what we do, every damn day of the week."

CHAPTER 11

AFTER BREAKFAST THE next morning, Jason Tyler asks Teresa if she and the family would like to go for a shopping trip, and Lance is pleased by how quickly she accepts the offer. Their discussion from last night hasn't been mentioned once since he and Teresa have woken up, and that's fine with Lance.

Now they are at a Super Stop & Shop and Jason is parking the Yukon at a distance from the store, where no other vehicles are parked near them. Sam says, "Boy, why couldn't we park closer? There are lots of spaces up front."

Jason says, "It'll give you a chance to get some exercise."

He gets out of the car, and Lance studies him, now knowing better. He sees how the man works. He wants their Yukon isolated, so it's easy to find—not easy for anyone to sneak up on it.

Their bodyguard also insists that they depart the Yukon one at a time: Lance, Teresa, Sam, and, last, Sandy. Back at their rental home, Jason had insisted that they enter the Yukon in the opposite order, Sandy going first and Lance bringing up the rear.

He shepherds them quickly across the parking lot and Lance feels relaxed amid the other shoppers out on this spring morning. It's pure America, with the shopping carts, aisle displays, and families of all ages and colors crowding around, and Lance looks to Jason to see if he's finally relaxed as well.

No, he's not. The man is with them, moving constantly, going forward, bringing up the rear, always looking around, always… guarding.

Always guarding. What a life that man must have.

They spend some time going slowly up and down the crowded aisles, and near the dairy coolers, Teresa abruptly stops and says, "Oh, dear, yogurt, that's worth stocking up on."

She moves around and starts handing containers to Lance, who in turn puts them in the cart, and he looks up and—

The kids are gone.

Jason is gone.

What the hell?

Teresa sees him stop and says, "What's the problem?"

"The kids have left. And so has Jason."

His wife looks around the bustling aisles and says, "You know those two. They probably decided to see if they could sneak away from Jason and us. I wouldn't worry."

Lance hears what she says, but, based on the look on her face and in her eyes, neither of them believes what she's saying.

CHAPTER 12

A FEW MINUTES later, he and Teresa are in the produce section of the supermarket. Teresa is doing her best to appear calm, and Lance is acting similarly placid. The to-and-fro of the safe shoppers, the long counters overflowing with fruit and vegetables…Lance finds it hard to believe that just a number of days ago, he and his family were in the middle of the Tunisian desert, living on canned goods and freeze-dried food.

A woman with dark-blue hair and yoga pants that are two sizes too small smashes into the side of Teresa's cart, shrugs, and walks off, and Teresa says, "This is an okay place, but, damn, I miss my Mollie Stone's from back home."

"Me, too," he says quietly, eyes shifting back and forth, "but my waistline isn't complaining about not getting those breakfast pastries. Hey, I saw you working this morning before we left. How's the guidebook coming along?"

Teresa starts examining yellow peaches with studied nonchalance, one at a time, constantly scanning the crowd for the kids. From long practice, Lance holds open a plastic bag. "How do you think?" she says. "No internet means no research. Without the great God of Google, it's like we've been tossed back in time thirty years…but at least I'm not pounding out my copy on a Remington typewriter. And your work?"

"Not good," he says. "After the time it took to get the permits and paperwork in place to get to the dig site, then leaving the dig nearly two months early…no matter the excuse, it's going to tick off Stanford pretty seriously when they get word. It'll knock my research back at least a year, if not longer."

Lance ties the plastic bag, gently places it in the shopping cart, and there's another bump as Teresa's cart hits the corner of a banana display. She mutters something and her face flushes, and Lance eyes the nearby vegetables and tries to lighten the mood.

He picks up a long, thick cucumber, shows it to his wife. "Hey, hon, does this remind you of anyone you know? Except for the color, I mean."

A wry smile that warms his heart. Teresa takes it from his hand, tosses it back, and puts a smaller pickling cucumber in his hand.

"I don't care if you've got your doctorate in archaeology, honey, you still don't know how to measure things."

He laughs and leans in for a kiss, but as he does so, Jason moves in unexpectedly, one hand on Sandy's shoulder, the other on Sam's. Sandy is reading a thick paperback almanac of current science facts, while her brother is holding a Batman comic book. Sam's not reading but squirming under the grasp of their bodyguard.

"Mom, Dad, do I have to listen to Jason?" he asks, voice loud. "He says I have to do what he tells me. Do I have to do that? Do I?"

Teresa stands still, both hands tight on the shopping cart handle. Lance notes the determined face of Jason and the angry face of his boy and thinks, *You have no idea, son*. Aloud he says, "Yes, at least for a while longer."

Sam squirms away. "How long is that? Huh? How long?"

Jason gives a not-so-gentle tap on Sam's shoulder. "Listen to your father."

Teresa reaches over, takes the almanac and comic book from her children's hands, puts them in the shopping cart, and continues her determined pushing and shopping.

Outside in the sunlit day, Lance moves along through the parking lot with his family and Jason. Sandy is reading her new almanac again and Sam is looking down at the ground, holding his Batman comic in his hands.

Jason opens the rear of the Yukon and helps Teresa put the groceries inside.

Lance is about to ask her what's for dinner when it happens.

On the other side of the parking lot comes a loud *bang!* Even though Lance sees every motion, every second, he still can't believe how fast Jason moves. The near rear door of the Yukon is thrown open and Sandy and Sam are literally tossed in. Lance races to the front passenger door, but by the time he opens it, his wife is already in the rear with the kids. The doors are shut and Jason has started up the Yukon, driving ahead with the driver's side door open.

Nervous, Lance asks, "What's going on—"

"Quiet!" Jason barks out, and from the rear, Teresa says, "It's okay, it's okay, it looks like a fender bender, that's all."

Lance swivels in his seat, looks back, sees a light-blue VW Beetle with its side caved in by a red Volvo station wagon backing out of its spot. He shakes his head. He can't believe the two things he has just seen.

One was how quick, efficient, and focused Jason was in getting all of them safely into the Yukon. It had been parked such that they could easily leave the parking lot and get on the main road.

And the other…the other was his wife, Teresa.

How she was looking at Jason with thanks, admiration…

And something else?

Just to punctuate that thought, Teresa reaches forward, pats Jason on his big right shoulder.

"Thanks, Jason," she says. "Thanks for looking out for us."

Then she sits back without having said a word to her husband.

CHAPTER 13

NEW YORK STATE Trooper Leonard Brooks reluctantly approaches the Second Precinct building of the Nassau County Police Department. The one-story brick station house, which provides coverage for Levittown, looks more like a bank branch.

Even though he's in full uniform, he's here on a personal mission, nothing to do with his work, and he's wondering what kind of reception he's going to get. After spending a couple of minutes in the lobby, he's escorted back into an office area and meets with Mark Crosby, a heavyset man with black hair who serves as both deputy commander and deputy inspector for the precinct.

Crosby leans over his clean desk and says, "All right, what can we do for you today, Trooper Brooks?"

His round campaign hat is in his lap, and he says, "It's delicate."

Crosby gives a knowing smile. "It always is. What do you have going on?"

"It's about my cousin," he says. "Teresa Sanderson. Her mother is concerned. She was overseas on a trip and wasn't due back for at least two months. But her mother got a disturbing phone call from her two weeks ago."

"How disturbing?"

"She told her mother that she was okay, and that she was stateside, and that she was staying in Levit…and then she was cut off."

"Levit? That's all?"

"That's all," Leonard says. "The phone call was disconnected, but her mother thinks she was going to say Levittown."

"Uh-huh," Crosby says, tapping fingers on his desk. "Does she have any friends or relatives here?"

"No."

"Do you know if she's ever traveled here before?"

"No."

"Any connections whatsoever?"

"Not that I'm aware of," Leonard says, knowing this conversation isn't going well. "All I'm asking is that if you could put the word out to your officers, keep a lookout for her, and—"

Crosby raises his hand. "Where's her home address?"

"Palo Alto, California."

"Have you contacted the police there?"

"Yes, but—"

Crosby shakes his head. "Troop L covers this part of the state. Are you in Troop L?"

"No, sir."

"Yet here you are," Crosby says. "Unofficially."

"Well, it's a favor, I guess, and—"

"What troop are you in, exactly?" Crosby asked, brows furrowed.

"Troop T, sir."

"Troop T! So you work on the Thruway, and you come here,

looking for a favor like that? Christ, if you were in Troop L, maybe I could be convinced to work something out, but nope. Not going to go out on a limb for you and your cousin. I don't know you, I don't know what you're up to."

"But if I—"

"You're wasting my time, Trooper Brooks. And I don't have enough of it. I think it's time for you to head on back to the Thruway before I make a phone call to your superior and tell 'em you've gone rogue. I don't think you'll like that, am I right?"

Leonard gets up, knowing his appointment is over. "You're very right, Inspector Crosby. I appreciate your time."

Crosby stays seated behind his desk and holds both hands up. "Look. These things work out, okay? I'm sure your cousin and her kids are fine."

"I hope you're right."

Back outside in the bright sun, Leonard Brooks adjusts his campaign hat and thinks through the conversation as he approaches his dark-blue Dodge Charger State Police cruiser. He opens the door.

Fruitful, but probably not in the way the good inspector had intended.

How had the man known his cousin had children?

CHAPTER 14

HELEN IS TAKING away an empty cup of tea from the nearby coffee table when Ronald Temple sees the black GMC Yukon pull into the driveway. The big guy gets out first and then opens the door. The adult male and female step out, followed by the young boy and the young girl. He escorts them into the house and a few minutes pass, and then the big guy comes back and takes several plastic bags of groceries into the house.

Helen comes back to wipe the table and Ronald says, "Do you see that? Do you? They all go as a group. Who in hell goes shopping as a group? And with a bodyguard as well?"

Helen rubs the table carefully with a soft cloth. "How do you know he's a bodyguard? Maybe he's just a friend. Or a relative. A brother of the man or woman."

Ronald picks up his binoculars, looks over at the house. He spots the woman putting groceries away in the refrigerator.

"I just know," he says, binoculars still up to his eyes. "When I was on the job, before going into security, you knew these things. Instinct. You could tell by the way somebody was walking that they were carrying a concealed weapon. That guy's carrying. I just know it."

Helen loses her patience before she leaves the living room. "Then for God's sake, call the police."

"Huh?" he asks, lowering the binoculars and turning his head.

"You heard me," she says, dishcloth still in her hand. "If you think that man over there is carrying a gun, and probably an illegal one, then call the police. Have them check it out...otherwise, Ronald, I'm getting tired of all of your conspiracy theories. Please."

Ronald feels his face warm. "Okay, that's what I'm going to do. Hand me the phone. I'll call the cops right now."

CHAPTER 15

LANCE HELPS TERESA put the groceries away. She frowns as she sits back at the round kitchen table with her books and laptop. "Once more, trying to write a book in the twenty-first century without using twenty-first-century technology."

He kisses the top of her head and says, "Just a couple more days. That's all."

She reaches up, squeezes his hand. "All right, professor, but if we get to day three and I'm still cut off from Google, you're going to be cut off from something more intimate. Got it?"

He kisses her once more. "Got it."

Lance takes a short walk down the near hallway and sees that Sandy is reading a thick textbook he lent her yesterday. Then he pokes his head into Sam's room. He's bent over a slowly developing dinosaur model.

Lance goes back into the hallway and nearly bumps into Jason.

"Professor," he says.

"Jason," he replies, remembering with a sour feeling a talk he'd had with Teresa last night. "Look...can we talk somewhere?"

Jason says, "Sure. Where?"

Good question. The only rooms not being used at the moment

were the tiny bathroom, the small living room, and the master bedroom. "Come with me, will you?"

Lance walks into the master bedroom and Jason follows him. Lance says, "I want to help."

Jason pauses for a second and says, "You can help me by staying together with your family, under my watch, until Langley's ready to move you. That will be very helpful."

"You don't understand," Lance says. "I'm the head of the household. I'm responsible for them, I'm responsible for them being in trouble and for being here, undercover. I want to help defend them if...if things happen."

Jason's face is impassive. "You ever serve? You ever been a cop? You an NRA member?"

"No to all three, but that doesn't mean I can't—"

And Lance can't believe how quickly Jason moves, because in a second or two, a black pistol has been pulled from somewhere in his clothing and is now in his right hand.

Time stands still. The pistol is pointing right at Lance's chest.

And without warning, Jason abruptly tosses the pistol at Lance.

Lance fumbles and catches it, almost dropping it along the way. The gun is cold and unfamiliar in his hand. It's bulky, ungainly, and it's the first time he's ever held a pistol in his life. The sense of power, the potential of being able to shoot, wound, and kill, practically emanates from the shape of the weapon.

"Shoot me," Jason says.

"What?"

"Shoot me." Jason steps forward: big, bulky, scary-looking.

"You've got the pistol. I'm threatening you, your wife, your kids…react! Shoot me! Now!"

Lance starts fumbling with the pistol, and in a quick snap, Jason takes it back, twisting two of Lance's fingers. He cries out.

"I don't have the time or the inclination to train you in self-defense, Professor Sanderson," Jason says, his voice filled with contempt. "You're out of your league. So keep your family together and let me do my job."

Lance feels ashamed, flustered, and doesn't know what to say.

And then the doorbell rings.

The pistol in Jason's hand disappears back under his clothes.

"Lockdown, now," he says in a commanding voice, and goes out, heading to the children's rooms. "Move."

CHAPTER 16

FROM HIS COMFORTABLE Barcalounger—he has a brief, grim thought that he'll probably be buried with this thing when the time comes—Ronald looks on with satisfaction as a Nassau County police cruiser slowly glides to a stop in front of the house next door.

"I'll be damned," he whispers, smiling. "They're actually going to do something."

He had made the call about ten minutes ago. Due to the bored response of the dispatcher—"Yeah, yeah" was her favorite phrase—Ronald didn't think anything was going to happen.

Sometimes it's nice to be proven wrong.

The cruiser door opens up and a female police officer steps out. Ronald gets up from his chair, grimacing from the pain in his legs. Taking his nostril tubes out, he slowly walks to the door, blanket and revolver in his hand.

From the kitchen comes the noise of a television, volume turned up loud. Helen is watching one of her favorite reality shows, about overdressed housewives yelling at each other. At the moment, they are baking a cake for an upcoming church function.

He goes to the front door and slowly opens it up. Near the

door is a small green oxygen tank with two wheels on its base and a handle—for use on those few occasions he steps outside. He drapes the hose around his head, turns the handle, and breathes in through his nostrils.

Despite all his ailments, he feels pretty good, watching the police officer approach the door, now partially hidden by a holly bush.

A thought from his past comes to him. This time…this time he won't screw up.

Tuesday, September 11, 2001.

He should have been at work that morning as a security officer for an investment firm, but the night before he had gotten hammered at Frank Watson's retirement bash. With a thudding hangover, he had called in sick, had switched off the phone, and had tumbled back to bed to sleep it off.

It had been hours before he realized what had happened and days before he received the list of dead people from his firm. Then the whispers came to him, followed him, and never went away for more than a decade and a half:

If you had been there, you could have saved some of them. Instead, you stayed home and slept it off. Useless drunk. Those people depended on you and you let them down.

He opens the door wider, preparing himself to provide backup for that solitary cop next door.

This time he's ready.

If something happens—and a part of him hopes it does—he won't be a failure for a second time.

In a way, he almost wishes things would go wrong, so he could prove himself.

He takes the revolver out from behind the blanket and holds it at his side.

CHAPTER 17

OFFICER KAREN GLYNN of the Nassau County Police Department wishes her shift was over so she could get home and do what she really wants to do, which is study up so she can apply to the New York City Police Department. Nothing against Nassau County and this dull suburb of Levittown, but she wants to do something serious as a cop, not track down stolen bicycles or take reports on vandalized mailboxes.

She pulls her white cruiser with its blue-and-orange stripes in front of the small blue house—the house that is supposedly harboring a man who might or might not be carrying a firearm, and who may or may not have a concealed pistol permit.

Biggest call of the week, she thinks, as she calls into dispatch that she's arrived. She opens the cruiser's door, walks up to the front of the house.

Clean and tidy, like every other house on this street, like practically every other house in this part of Nassau County, and she rings the doorbell once, twice, and steps back as the door opens.

"Yes?" the man at the door asks. "Can I help you, officer?"

Karen steps back one more time, body on automatic, examining the bulky guy, and she goes into full alert. Even though he's well-dressed and his hands are empty, it's those eyes…

"Ah, yes," she says. "Officer Glynn, Nassau County Police Department. I'm investigating a…complaint."

"What kind of complaint, officer?"

She says, "Can I see some identification, please?"

A second or two passes, feeling like an hour. He smiles. "Of course." His right hand slowly goes to his pocket and her throat is dry, her hand is on her holster, and he comes back with a wallet, from which he pulls out a driver's license.

"Here," he says. "Will this do?"

She takes the license, gives it a very quick glance—Karen doesn't want to lose focus on this hulk in front of her—and returns it. "Thank you, Mister Tyler. I see that license is from Virginia. Can I ask why you're here in Levittown?"

"Visiting," he says evenly.

"I see," she says. "Well, the department has received word that you've been seen walking off the premises, carrying a concealed weapon. Is that true?"

"Word from whom?"

"Is that true? That you're carrying a concealed weapon?"

Hesitation, then the slightest of nods. "That's true."

"Do you have a concealed carry permit, Mister Tyler?"

"I do."

"May I see it, please?"

Another second that seems to drag on and on.

He looks at her.

"Yes," he says. "It's here in my wallet as well."

And another plastic-embossed card is removed and passed over, with the man's photo on it, and issued from Nassau County.

Karen gives it a glance, passes it back.

All in order.

Still…

Why is her heart racing so?

"May I come in?" she asks.

"Why?"

"Because I'd like to take a look around."

A slight smile that looks as dangerous as the bared teeth of a lunging German shepherd being held back only by a thin and fraying rope. "I don't think so."

"Why?"

"Because."

Karen is now convinced that even though this guy has all the right permits and identification, something strange is definitely going on, and she starts to—

He says, "Is this when you're going to say you're going to come in now, or go to a helpful judge to get a search warrant for some sort of malfeasance, imagined or otherwise?"

"I, uh—"

The man says, "Perhaps this might help."

The wallet is returned to his pants, and he reaches into another pocket, removes a business-sized envelope, folded in half, and removes a thick white piece of stationery, which Karen holds and reads and then reads one more time.

She nods. Mouth still very, very dry.

Passes the piece of paper back.

"Thanks… I, uh, I'll be heading out. Thanks for your cooperation."

"Glad to do it, Officer Glynn," he says, and he gently closes the door in front of her.

Karen turns and goes back to her cruiser, reviewing what she has just seen: a letter signed by both the governor and the president, asking the reader of said letter to give every courtesy and consideration to its bearer, one Jason Tyler of Arlington, Virginia.

Whatever the hell is going on here is way, way above her pay grade, and she wants none of it.

She stops at her cruiser and an old man approaches her, yelling.

Christ on a crutch, she thinks, this day just keeps getting loopier by the second.

CHAPTER 18

RONALD TEMPLE WAITS and watches, waits and watches, and—

The police officer heads back toward her cruiser.

Alone.

Not calling for backup? Not dragging that big guy out to the cruiser in handcuffs?

Unbelievable!

He drops his blanket and revolver on the floor, grabs his oxygen tank handle, and starts out of the door.

The oxygen tank rattling behind him, he goes across the lawn, seeing the female officer reach her cruiser.

"Hey!" he calls out, ashamed at how weak his voice is. "Hey! Officer! Over here!"

She opens the door to her cruiser, hesitates just for a moment.

Long enough.

"Hey…what's going on here?" he asks, wheezing to a halt, the tank beside him. "Why are you leaving so soon?"

The police officer is cool, polite, and uncooperative, and Ronald remembers the times he behaved the same way when he was on the job.

"Are you the neighbor who made the complaint?" she asks.

"I did." His breathing is harsh, and he feels like a series of explosive coughs are about to rip from his lungs.

"It was unfounded."

"What?"

"Sir, it was unfounded."

He walks to her, stops as he forgets his wheeled oxygen tank. The tubes rip from his nose, the tank falling over. "What do you mean, unfounded? I saw it! Hey, I was on the job for twenty-plus years, back in Manhattan, and I know what the hell I'm talking about."

The female officer shakes her head again. "Sir, it was unfounded...and if you'll excuse me, I have to go back on patrol."

That's it. She's back in her cruiser. The engine starts right up, and in a few seconds, the cruiser makes a left-hand turn and is gone.

Ronald is alone on the empty street.

But he senses something.

He slowly moves, breathing hard, toward his oxygen tubes on the grass, his oxygen bottle on its side.

There.

The large man in the house...he's at the door.

It's open.

He's staring right at Ronald.

Right at him.

So now he knows who made the call.

Who told the police all about him.

The stare is quiet, unmoving, unyielding.

Ronald feels that old fear of being alone out on the street, no partner, no backup. He suddenly wishes the unhelpful officer from Nassau County was still here, with her cruiser and her radio.

It's been a very long time since Ronald has been this afraid.

CHAPTER 19

TERESA SANDERSON SITS on the crowded bathroom floor with her legs pulled up to her and her arms wrapped around her knees, trying not to shiver with fear. Lance is next to her, arm around her shoulders. Her children are huddled in the bathtub, a heavy and bulky black Kevlar blanket draped over the two of them. Jason had moved quickly, putting Sandy in first, then her brother on top of her, and putting the blanket in place. Another Kevlar blanket is attached to the locked bathroom door behind them.

The bathroom is a dump. Filthy tile, a dirty tub, a leaking faucet over an old porcelain sink, and a toilet that flushes itself every now and then, usually at three in the morning. Over the toilet is a small window, so dirty that the outside can't be clearly seen. There's a handmade crooked shelf that holds some cleaning supplies, most of them almost as old as Sam.

Lance notes Teresa's review of the dingy bathroom and gently leans into her.

"Honey?" he asks.

"Yes?"

"I love what you've done with the place." His smile warms her and she leans back into him.

Still…

How in God's name did she end up here, in danger, with her kids and her husband? What combination of forces and coincidences have conspired to do this to her and her family?

Risk.

Always a matter of risk, but long before, when Sam and Sandy were just barely toddlers, she wanted to go along with Lance as he dove into the past, unlocking the secrets of Carthage and its long-standing enemy, Rome. It had all worked out from the start. She spent quality time with her husband, and her kids had grown up knowing there was more to the world than just a school playground and computer games.

She strains to listen to what's happening on the other side of the door. A murmur of voices, that's all.

Now?

Now she regrets it all, and though she hates to admit it, she regrets trusting Lance. Oh, he's a solid husband, smart, funny, and loyal, good in bed and good at taking care of the kids. But sometimes…sometimes he is caught in the past, thinking of battles involving Carthage and Rome instead of lifting his head and seeing the battles going on around them.

She shifts her weight, still listening.

Because this is a battle that has caught up to her and her family.

She thinks about their time in Tunisia, and with guilt flooding through her, she remembers one thing that she's been hiding from Lance and Jason and the other government people they've encountered since their abrupt departure.

About that day in the nearest city, Bizerte, when she had been taking photographs in the marketplace.

Three hard-looking men had been sitting at a café table, drinking coffee, and she loved the way the light was coming in past the overhanging tapestries. She had taken the photo, and the men—suddenly and scarily angry—had leapt as one from the table and chased her through the crowds.

Who were they? Why didn't they want their photos taken?

Teresa knows…though she's too scared to admit it, even now.

She had never told Lance about what had happened. She had planned to tell him the next day, but on that next day—

A knock on the bathroom door makes her jump.

"Sanderson family." It's the familiar voice of Jason. "Sanderson family, we are clear."

She untangles herself from Lance's grasp and gets up. Lance unlocks the bathroom door. Teresa goes over to the bathtub and pulls away the heavy Kevlar blanket, her heart breaking when she sees her boy and her girl scared and huddled in the bottom of the tub.

Jason comes in, going past Lance, helping out Sam and then Sandy. "You okay, kids?" he asks.

"I need to go back to my reading," Sandy announces. "I've wasted nine minutes in here."

Sam says, "And she farts. And won't say she's sorry."

Sam barrels out and his older sister follows him, and Jason says, "All clear."

Lance nods in satisfaction, but Teresa can't stand it. "All

clear? For now…but for how long? Will we ever be safe, ever again, will we?"

The two men look away from her and say nothing.

And she wishes she was brave enough to tell them what she's thinking: that this is all her fault.

CHAPTER 20

TWO BLOCKS AWAY from Perry Street in downtown Trenton, New Jersey, Gray Evans locks his rental car in front of a boarded-up three-story brick building, one of at least six he sees up and down this side street. The streets are filthy, the streetlights are broken, and the sidewalks are cracked and have knee-high weeds growing out of them.

Gray glances up and down the street. A thin black dog trots along the other side of the street, disappears into a narrow alley. Gray takes a deep breath, smells the familiar scents he's encountered over the years in different parts of the world, and knows where he is: a place where people and the government have given up. Lead-tainted water, uncollected trash, decaying buildings. All the signs of a collapsing civilization.

He walks up a block, takes a right. Another series of three-story brick buildings, but the one at the end has lights on and is a bodega. Two bars are across the street, lights on, some men walking in, others stumbling out with drink-fueled vigor. Shouts, music, and more shouts punctuate the night.

At the center of the block is a secure metal-frame door with re-inforced hinges and a keypad combination lock. He punches in eight numbers he's memorized, turns the knob, and enters a different world. The floor is covered in clean tile and the lights are all on. There's a narrow elevator in front of him—again, with a keypad lock. He punches in another set of numbers, the door glides open, he gets in, and the elevator gently takes him up to the third floor.

It opens up into a wide, open loft with recessed lighting. There's a grouping of comfortable leather furniture in front of him, a kitchen to the right with stainless steel appliances, and a wide work area in the distance consisting of a conference table, four large-screen monitors, banks of servers with blinking lights, and two computer workstations.

A man leaning on a cane approaches him, smiling, holding out his right hand. "Gray. On time, as always."

"That's how I roll, Abraham."

"Come on in."

Abraham leads him to the conference table. He has on leather moccasins, khaki slacks, and a Yankees T-shirt. He's in his early thirties, with trimmed black hair, a black goatee, and gold earrings in each ear.

He settles down and Gray sits across from him. Abraham says, "Refreshments?"

"Not now," Gray says.

"Suit yourself," Abraham says, sitting still, his cane tight in his left hand. "What do you need?"

Gray says, "Looking for the Sanderson family. Husband and wife, Lance and Teresa. Preteen daughter and son, Sandy and Sam.

All from Palo Alto. Hubby is a professor at Stanford, wife is a free-lance author, has written two travel guides. A couple of weeks ago they were in Tunisia. Now I think they're in Levittown."

"From Tunisia to Levittown, what a letdown," Abraham says.

"I guess."

"You want them found?"

"Very much so," Gray says.

"Usual fee?"

"Plus ten percent," Gray says. "Your skills...I think they deserve to be compensated."

"Glad to hear it."

"Plus I'm in a rush."

"You or your client?"

"What difference does it make?"

Abraham looks up at the open ceiling, where a red digital clock is suspended. "Let's say...twenty-four hours."

"Perfect."

Gray gets up and walks out.

He's never been one for extended good-byes.

Back to his rental car—Gray always purchases the extra insurance, just because of trips like these—he comes upon two local youths sitting on the hood. They're dressed in baggy pants with their underwear showing, wearing lots of gold chains—or bling, he can never keep up with latest trends—and baseball caps worn at an angle.

"Yo," the one on the left says, not moving. "Nice rig."

"Glad you like it," he says. "It's a rental."

The other youth says, "Rental or no, you owe us a parking fee."

"I do?" Gray asks, stepping closer. "Funny, I don't see any signs."

The first one says, "It's understood, bro. This place and all. It's…understood. We watched your rig, nothing happened to it, we get compensated."

Gray says, "Appreciate the concern, fellas, but I respectfully decline."

The first one gets off the car. "Bad move, bro. We're not taking no for an answer."

Gray eyes them both and says, "All right, here's the deal. Tell me what happened here in December 1776 and I'll let you go."

The second laughs. "You'll let us go?"

They both advance on him. The first one says, "Who the hell you think you are?"

Gray waits until the last moment, relaxed. Unless these two are well trained and exceptional, and know how to work as a team, they are quite vulnerable.

They just don't know it yet.

He spins and kicks hard at the right knee of the closest one, making him cry out and fall to the ground. His friend attempts to run away and Gray snags the waistband of his exposed underwear, gives it a severe tug—crushing whatever might be in the way—and spins him back so he falls against the hood of his rental.

The two youths are on the ground, moaning and clasping at their injured parts. Gray leans over and says, "Tell you who I am. I'm the guy who knows Washington and his troops saved the revolution here in Trenton, for the eventual benefit of you two dopes."

More moans and they scramble away in fear as Gray gets closer and says, "Guys?"

Neither one of them attempts to speak. Gray says, "Guys…I really need to go. Mind getting out of the way?"

And in seconds they're gone.

Gray gets into his rental and heads out.

It's been a full day.

CHAPTER 21

AFTER A THREE-HOUR run north from Levittown, New York State Trooper Leonard Brooks arrives in Latham—just north of Albany, New York—and parks his cruiser at the office building that houses the New York State Intelligence Center. Having called ahead, he gets a friendlier reception here than he had in Nassau County, and he is quickly ushered into a plain-looking office where he meets with Beth Draper, an intelligence analyst for the State Police.

She stands up from her desk, which is piled high with forms and folders, and comes around to give him a hug and a kiss on the cheek. "Brooksie, good to see you again."

"The same."

He sits down, feeling warm, thinking, *Oh, yes, much nicer reception than Levittown*. He and Beth dated for a year or so right after both of them graduated from the New York State Police Academy in Albany.

She had gone into intelligence and he had gone into patrol. They saw each other every few months or so and were now less than lovers and more than just friends.

Beth sits down, runs both hands through her long blond hair. She's wearing a plain white blouse and black slacks that fail to conceal her pretty curves. "Okay, it's past quitting time. Tell me what you need."

He spends the next few minutes explaining his search for his cousin, the lack of response from authorities in Palo Alto and Levittown, and how messages to Teresa's cell phone, home phone, and e-mail have all gone unanswered.

"Damn," she says. "Don't like the sound of that."

"Neither do I."

"What do you think?" she asks. "She have enemies? Her husband?"

"She's a freelance writer. He's an archaeologist. Not the enemy-making type."

"You'd be surprised. You said they were in North Africa recently?"

"Tunisia."

"The whole family?"

"Teresa…she's one of those granola types. Wants to expose her kids to the bigger world. And her husband…he's sort of an expert on Carthage."

"Car what?"

"Carthage. North African empire that were rivals of Rome until Rome crushed them. You've heard of Rome, haven't you?"

She smiles, a perfect little smile of white teeth that still stirs him. "Sure. Rome. About ninety minutes away. Where the Erie Canal was started. Please stop busting my chops, Brooksie."

"Chop-busting done."

Beth sighs, scribbles a few things on a piece of scrap paper. "I'll do what I can, I'll start sniffing around…but you should prepare yourself."

His hands feel chilled, like a block of ice was suddenly nearby. "What are you saying?"

"What you already know, in your heart of hearts," Beth says, still writing. "Phone call unexpectedly broken off. No information from any authorities. Friends and relatives don't know where they are. Phone, cell phone, and e-mail all unanswered."

She looks up, pretty face solemn. "You remember the Petrov family, two years ago? On the run from the Russian mob? Hiding out?"

Leonard feels much cooler. "Yes."

Beth says, "It took one slipup…a postcard to a relative, saying all was well. And that's all." Beth pauses. "I hear that when the house was finally cleared by the FBI, they had to bulldoze it down to the foundation. Because they couldn't get all the bloodstains out of the floors and walls."

CHAPTER 22

SAM SANDERSON OPENS the door to his bedroom, checks out the hallway. All quiet. Lights off. Of course it would be quiet…this crappy place doesn't even have a television!

He closes the door, pops himself down on his unmade bed. He's got books, he's got dinosaur models…and he's bored.

God, he's so bored.

No television!

And there's no computer!

Oh, Mom has a laptop, but something inside the computer has been switched off, meaning it can't be used to access the internet.

So Sam can't do research on which new dinosaur models he wants to order, he can't check out the dinosaur forums he loves to poke around in, and he can't e-mail…about a half-dozen of his buds back in California must be wondering why he hasn't answered them.

Great. When he finally gets back to Palo Alto, his friends will think he's been a jerk because he hasn't answered their e-mails.

Plus…he reaches into his jeans pocket, tugs out a piece of metal and plastic, rolls it around in his fingers. This is something he picked up back at that desert place, something he hadn't shown Dad. It wasn't one of those broken bowl pieces, for sure…it looked too new. So what is it?

He puts it back in his pocket. If he had a computer that really worked, he could find out…

Sam bounces off the bed, opens the door one more time. Still dark, still quiet. He wonders where Jason is hiding. Ever since they left Tunisia, that scary bad guy has been hanging with them, day after day. Sam knows something bad happened back in Tunisia, but why should he have to pay for it?

He can't go anywhere alone, he can't go play in the yard by himself, and no computer…

Man, he's bored!

He closes the door and tries to tiptoe back to his bed.

Bored or not, he has a plan.

This crappy house has a house to the left and one to the right. The one to the left has some snoopy old guy who keeps on peeking in at them with binoculars. But the other house…there's a guy and girl who live there together, and the funny thing is, they both work at night.

Which means that, right now, their house is empty.

The house he can see through his bedroom window.

And he knows they use a computer…because he can see them working on it in their living room.

Sam knows something else, too.

The other day the two of them came back from some errand, and he saw the woman dig and dig through her purse, and then the guy laughed at her and removed a brick from the steps, took out a key, and unlocked the front door.

So the house over there is empty.

The house that has a computer.

And he knows where the key to the door is hidden.

Sam goes to the window, opens up the lock, and slides the window open, and then the screen. It makes a squeaky noise.

He waits.

And waits.

No one seems to have heard him.

Good!

He clambers outside and steps on the grass and then starts to the empty house.

If he's very, very lucky, he'll be on the computer in just a few minutes, and no one will ever, ever know.

CHAPTER 23

LANCE SANDERSON TOSSES and turns, Teresa deeply asleep next to him.

He admires his wife in so many ways, including how she can instantly drop off to sleep. She'll be reading a magazine or a book and will then put her reading material down, give Lance a quick kiss, and say, "Night, honey. I'm off to sleep."

And within a minute, she will be deep asleep.

Oh, to have that power!

He stares up at the ceiling. Memories come back to him, the memory of that last full day in Tunisia, when everything went wrong.

The dig site is three years old, about fifty or so kilometers from the famed ruins of Carthage, which are situated near Tunis, the capital of Tunisia. It is in a remote section of a desert near the P11 highway, and Lance and his graduate students, along with local laborers, are excavating an estate that may or may not have belonged to a prominent Carthaginian official before the Romans sacked the city in 146 BC.

On this day the sun is overhead and very bright. His two graduate students from Stanford, young men who still have the vigor and enthusiasm he remembers from his own grad school days, are gone off to a day's worth of errands to the nearby port city of Bizerte. Teresa and Sam are under a flapping canvas tarpaulin, cataloguing and photographing some of the artifacts—coins, broken pottery, cooking vessels—that he and his crew have recovered. Teresa has been quiet this morning, only saying she has something to discuss with him later at the morning break, and he puts it out of his mind. Poor honey is probably still upset at the stench coming from their shared chemical toilets.

And Sandy? Lance smiles to himself. Sandy is Sandy, sitting in a corner on a folding camp chair, reading and reading, ignoring her surroundings, only bestirring herself to find something new to read.

The surroundings are familiar to Lance after years of work, digging and cataloguing: carefully dug square pits, grid lines set up with strings and white tape. Some of the laborers are bent over at work, with Karim, the cheerful site supervisor, overlooking it all. A couple of bored militiamen carrying AK-47s sit under their own small tents and sip tea all day long.

There had been the briefest tussle earlier over the pay, but that had been quickly settled via the most common North African economic practice—haggling.

Lance takes a long swig of water from his own canteen, starts walking down to the excavation site to see how the latest dig area is proceeding. A wall had been found two days ago.

And he looks up to the tent and—

Sam and Teresa are bent over a long wooden table, both examining a piece of pottery that may or may not be from Greece, and—

Where's Sandy?

Where's his little girl?

He whips his head around. The dig site is mostly flat, except for a line of hills about a hundred meters away. A dirt road to the main collection of tents leads off to a poorly paved road that leads to the government highway, and—

If Sandy is anywhere near here, he would be able to pick her out immediately.

But she's missing.

"Sandy!" he yells.

He starts running to the tent, as Teresa looks up, her face frozen in fear.

"Sandy!"

And a scream wakes him up.

He's in Levittown.

Teresa is sitting up next to him.

The screaming goes on and on.

Teresa leaps out of bed, saying, "Oh, God, it's Sandy!"

Lance races out of the bedroom, right behind his wife.

CHAPTER 24

SAM SANDERSON FEELS like a ninja or a secret agent, sneaking across the side lawn, going up to the other house. The grass is wet from the evening dew and he scampers up to the front door. It's easy to see because of the streetlights and lights from the other houses in this boring place.

He goes up to the brick steps, tugs at one of the bricks, then another, and, yes, the third brick is the one! It comes free, and he pokes his hand in and comes up with a key, attached to a small piece of string.

There.

He goes up to the door, looks around, opens up the storm door, puts the key in the lock, and…

Yep.

He's inside!

He steps in, trying to be quiet, and he remembers to close the door behind him. For just a moment he feels scared, guilty, but it passes. The neighbors are gone, everything's quiet back at the other house, and he just wants to get in long enough to go online for a while.

Sam walks into a place that smells new and clean, unlike the dump they're living in. He doesn't mind camping out, like they were doing in Tunisia, but that place back there…ugh.

He goes through a wide and clean kitchen, and there, on a table in a little nook, is a laptop hooked up to a large-screen display. A couple of night-lights are on, and the light over the stove is lit up as well, meaning it's clear going.

He sits in the big chair, scoots forward, and smiles. The computer is a MacBook Pro. Just like the one he has back home in California. Sweet!

Sam powers it up and the screen flickers to life, starting with the Apple logo, and then the desktop comes into view, and, along with everything else, there's the little icon for Safari, the Apple web browser.

Double-click there, and Google comes up, and maybe he should figure out what that piece of metal and plastic is that's in his pocket, but, no, that's for later. He types in his Gmail account, and signs in, and…

Score!

Look at that.

He's in.

Wow.

It's been a long, long time…

He starts tapping, answering one e-mail and then another, and then there's one from his best bud, Toby, and he writes to him, *Toby, you won't believe what's going on and it's been some scary shit, and believe it or not, I flew on my first helicopter ride and…*

Sam stops typing.

He feels like something weird is going on.

Was that a noise out there?

Or a light?

He finishes the e-mail, sends it, shuts down the computer, and starts out of the house.

Darn it, he wanted to spend at least an hour here, but now…

He's scared now.

Scared of being caught.

Suppose the man or the woman who lives here, suppose one of them got sick?

And they came back home right now? With him in the house?

How could he explain that?

Sam stops at the door, peers out.

The driveway's still empty.

Good.

Maybe…

Well, he could go back. He was just scared. That's all.

A wuss.

But still…

Maybe he could come back tomorrow night, now that he's done it once already.

He steps out, locks the door, puts the key back under the loose brick, and, again, like a ninja or a secret agent, he races across the lawn, back to where he's supposed to be.

A shadow comes toward him and he screams and is tossed to the ground.

CHAPTER 25

IT'S A RACE down the hallway outside of their bedrooms and Teresa wins it, bursting into Sandy's bedroom. She's standing at the foot of the bed, screaming, wearing a long Winnie-the-Pooh nightshirt and in bare feet, and Teresa scoops up her daughter and Lance says, "What's wrong? What's wrong? Did you have a bad dream?"

His wife picks up on what he's just said, and she kisses the top of her head, stroke's Sandy's hair, and says, "It's okay, honey, it's okay. Was it a bad dream? Was it a bad dream?"

Sandy squirms free from her mother's grasp. She's panting so hard that she's almost hyperventilating, and she says, "The bad man got Sam! The bad man got Sam! The bad man got Sam!"

Lance goes out of Sandy's room, opens the door to Sam's.

It's empty.

"Sam!" he yells. "Sam!"

The bedroom window is open. Lance strides forward, leans his hands on the sill, pokes his head out. "Sam, you out there?"

Teresa comes in, holding Sandy by her shoulders as she stands before her mother. The young girl has stopped screaming. Her face is red and is set. "Is he here? Is he?"

"No."

Lance goes out of Sam's room, goes into the kitchen, the small living room, and—

No Sam.

"Sam!"

He checks the bathroom.

Empty.

Teresa comes up, still holding Sandy.

"Where is he?"

"I don't know."

"And…where's Jason?"

Lance is stunned. How in God's name had he missed *that*?

"Jason! Where are you?"

Teresa's eyes well up. "Lance…what's going on? Where are they?"

A loud slamming noise startles them all, and Lance steps back as the rear door to the little house flies open. Jason strides in, face screwed up with fury, dragging young Sam in by his T-shirt collar.

CHAPTER 26

GRAY EVANS IS stretched out on a hotel bed, relaxed, comfortable, with a woman named Vanessa resting next to him on a pillow, looking at him, her finely manicured nails tracing circles on his chest.

"You doing okay?" she asks.

"Fine."

"You interested in more?"

"How much time do I have left?"

She raises herself up, revealing an impressive set of curves, pulls a length of red hair from her face, and checks out the clock radio.

"Another fifteen minutes. If you want."

She settles back down, and Gray remembers that old, old joke from way back: you don't pay a prostitute to stay, you pay her to leave when you're done.

Still…it was nice to have some female company for a while, to refresh and recharge his batteries before he resumes his job.

His iPhone starts ringing.

Vanessa says, "You want me to answer it?"

Gray gives her his best smile. "You want some broken fingers?"

He rolls off the bed, grabs his iPhone, goes into the bathroom. He looks back and says, "Stay on the bed, all right? That's what I'm paying you for, to do what I want…and I want you to stay on the bed."

She stretches and smiles and says not a word.

Inside the bathroom he turns on the faucet to help mask his voice, answers the phone, and it's Abraham, his researcher.

"Got a hit about ten minutes ago."

"Fantastic," Gray says. "Tell me more."

Abraham chuckles. "Over the open air? For real? I don't think so."

"Okay, I'll come over right now."

"Please…I'm going back to bed," Abraham says. "Come over tomorrow after nine a.m. and I'll give you the information."

"Solid?"

"As a rock."

Gray says, "Why don't I come over now?"

Abraham chuckles again. "I don't meet clients at night. You know that."

"Okay. I'll see you at 9:01 tomorrow."

"That's a date."

Gray hears the call disconnect and says to the dead air, "Oh, one more thing. Can you tell me where you got the hit from?"

No answer, of course, but he moves to the bathroom door and swings it open. He startles Vanessa, who's been standing right there, a hotel robe wrapped around her. Vanessa's eyes are wide and she looks like a little girl being caught doing something naughty by her teacher.

Gray smiles, steps by her, and goes to the hotel room door.

Makes sure it's locked.

Vanessa moves away from him, sits on the bed.

"Look—" she starts.

Gray puts a finger to his lips, shushing her. He switches on the television, finds an HBO movie, and boosts up the volume.

"Honey," he says, and then says the last words she will ever hear. "All I told you to do was to stay on the bed."

CHAPTER 27

LANCE CATCHES HIS breath. "Okay, what the hell is going on here?"

Jason propels Lance's son—his son!—forward into the kitchen and says, "I was outside, maintaining a surveillance position. Approximately fourteen minutes ago, I saw your son depart his bedroom via an open window."

Lance feels like his legs have just morphed into solid stone. "Sam, is that true?"

"Dad, he hurt me! He hurt my shoulder!"

Lance says, "Sam, did you sneak out? Did you?"

Sam is defiant. "I'm bored! I wanted to go outside. Is that a crime?"

"No," Lance says. "But we have to...we have to do things to stay safe."

Teresa has her arms around Sandy, whose face is cool and impassive. She says, "Your father is right, Sam. We have to...we have to stay together, to be safe."

Sam's face is still screwed up in young defiance, and Jason says, "There's more."

"More?" Lance asks. "What the hell do you mean by that?"

Jason is standing still and collected, like a military professional making a report. "Sir, after your son left the house, I observed him going to the Barnes' house."

Teresa says, "Who are the Barnes?"

Lance says, "The young couple that lives next door. Not the dirty old man."

"Dad—"

Lance says, "Go on, Jason."

"Sir, I observed your son go to the front steps of the Barnes' house. Apparently there is a house key hidden in the brick steps leading in. After retrieving the key, he gained entrance to the house."

Teresa put a hand to her mouth. "Sam!"

Lance says, "Hold on, you mean—"

Jason goes on, speaking over Lance. "After entering the house, I lost sight of your son. But I did see movement within, and I saw a computer being turned on. The glow and light were unmistakable. And I saw the outline of your son sitting in front of the computer. I then approached the house and the computer screen went dark, and your son exited."

The kitchen falls quiet. Lance stares at his boy, who blinks his eyes and looks away. Teresa is just quietly shaking her head. Jason catches Lance's eyes.

"Sir?"

Sandy speaks to her younger brother. "Sam, you've been naughty. I've told you to stop being naughty." And she falls quiet.

Lance says, "Sam…you know the rules. We…we can't go online. That's why Mom's laptop has been disabled. It's too dangerous."

Sam says, "I didn't do it."

Teresa says, "But Jason says he saw you."

Sam steps over and joins his mother and sister, looks back at Jason. "Yeah…I was there…but…I turned on the computer…and I waited…and I got scared. I remembered the rules. So I turned it off and ran outside."

Lance sees something strange going on with Jason's face, like he's wrestling with some struggle he can't vocalize.

He says, "Sam? Are you telling the truth?"

Sam says, "Yes! You know I am…you can trust me…"

Lance's heart aches. His boy…versus what Jason saw.

What to do?

Lance says, "Sam? Did you go online? Did you put us in danger?"

Jason still looks…guilty. The man looks guilty.

Sam says, "Dad…I didn't. Honest."

Another few seconds pass.

Lance says, "All right, I trust you, Sam. C'mon, let's get you to bed."

Teresa pats Sandy on her shoulders. "Yes…all of us, let's go to bed. And, Jason…thank you. Thank you for keeping us safe. Sam…" She tugs at his near ear, making him squirm. "I swear to God, you do anything like that, ever again, I'll break you. Got it?"

One last look at Jason. The man should be happy at being complimented by Teresa, but no.

He doesn't look happy at all.

CHAPTER 28

TWO HUNDRED SIXTY-FIVE miles to the southwest of Levittown, New York, in a quiet office building in a crowded suburban office park, a government employee named Williams yawns as he monitors newsfeeds from various cable networks from across the globe. One of the open secrets of the intelligence agencies in the United States is that they get the bulk of their emerging information the same way everyone else does: from television.

Williams yawns again. He has the overnight shift and hates it. He wants to make a difference, wants to fight extremism, and so far, all he's done is ruin his sleep patterns and watch too much television.

Damn, it's like he's back in college…

Except in college he had a better room.

This room is square, functional, with flickering overhead lights, and it's stuffy, like the air in here hasn't been refreshed since this new, disturbed millennium began years back.

His phone rings, and he sees it's the internal line, one that can only be accessed from within the building.

He picks it up. "Williams."

"This is Cauchon." A female voice. "Domestic observation."

"Go," Williams says, picking up a pen.

"We have a breach of internet protocol, for an individual named Sanderson, Samuel. Occurred thirty-seven minutes ago. He's under covert protection in Levittown, New York. Make the necessary notifications."

"Got it," Williams says.

He goes to his keyboard, goes through the department's intranet system, finds the covert protection order for SANDERSON, SAMUEL—a ten-year-old boy!—and notes who he needs to contact.

The guy known as "the Big Man."

He gains a secure outside line for his telephone system, calls the Big Man at home.

No answer.

He tries the Big Man's office.

No answer.

He calls the Big Man's personal handheld device, issued by the same group Williams works for.

It rings, rings, and then it's picked up.

"Sir, this is—"

The voice is a recording. "You know who this is. Leave the message. Off."

Williams clears his voice. "Sir, this is James Williams, calling from Department G-17. We have a breach of internet protocol for a...Sanderson, a Samuel Sanderson. This is your official notification."

He hangs up the phone, goes back to the protocol section. If he doesn't hear back from the Big Man within the hour, he is to dispatch a federal police unit to the Big Man's house and physically make the notification.

Then Williams looks up at the monitors.

CNN, MSNBC, and now Fox and some of the international cable stations are all broadcasting the same scene: a billowing cloud of black smoke and flames coming out from an Underground station in London.

Williams starts making other, more urgent notifications.

Within minutes, he has forgotten all about the ten-year-old boy and the Big Man.

CHAPTER 29

LANCE PUTS SAM to bed and closes and locks the window.

"Sam."

"Yes, Dad," he says, quiet and subdued.

"You…I know it's boring. It's boring for all of us. But you've got to listen to us, including Jason. You've got to do what you're told."

"Yes, Dad."

Lance goes to the door, turns off the light. "And this light remains off. Until it's time to get up."

"Yes, Dad."

"And tomorrow…sorry, you're confined to your room."

In the kitchen, Jason is making a cup of coffee, and there's an aura, a sense of danger in his tense shoulders as Lance passes him by. He knocks on the door to Sandy's room and she says, "Come in," and he goes in.

She's reading another one of his books and says, "I plan to read for another twelve minutes. Then I will shut the light off and go to sleep."

"That's good to know," he says. "You doing all right?"

Sandy says, "I do have a question, Dad."

"Okay."

His young daughter says, "When we left Tunisia, we were in a helicopter. Why didn't it crash?"

Lance is puzzled. "Sorry, honey, I don't understand the question."

She says, "I understand why aircraft fly. The theory of lift over the wings. That makes sense. But I don't understand helicopters. They don't make sense. They should crash."

Lance says, "We'll talk about it tomorrow, okay? I'll see what I can find."

"Okay, Dad."

He closes her door and stands for a moment in the hallway, remembering.

With Karim at his side, and with the other local workers fanning out, he and Teresa race around the dig site, frantically looking for their daughter, after he orders Sam to stay put.

Lance goes up along the hills on the near side of the camp, and Karim says, "Look! Look!"

Fresh, small footprints in the dirt.

And a few minutes later, he and Karim find Sandy, happily sitting in front of a small, open cave that is well hidden from view. Behind her, there are wooden and black plastic crates, piled up high on each other, and in a corner of the cave, one of the crates is open.

Revealing a tangled collection of RPG-7s, rocket-propelled grenade launchers.

"Sandy?" Lance asks, coming forward. "What are you doing?"

"I ran out of things to read back at camp," she says. "I'm reading now."

In a metal box near her that's been broken open, there are magazines, newspapers, and books, all in Arabic or French. Lance squats down, examines what she's reading, a thick pile of papers, printed on one side and loosely bound in a black binder.

Lance takes the binder out of her hand, his breathing quickening. "Honey, we've got to go."

"But I haven't finished reading."

He grabs his daughter, picks her up. Karim looks past them, at the boxes of weapons piled higher and deeper into the cave.

Karim's eyes are wide with fright. "Oh, Lance, this is bad. Very, very bad."

Lance starts out of the cave entrance, carrying Sandy, his breathing now labored and harsh.

"Oh, yes, very bad," Lance says. "Very bad."

CHAPTER 30

LANCE IS FINALLY in bed with Teresa, who nuzzles his neck, and he says, "Sandy...she asked me something odd."

"Oh, what's that?" she asks. "Did she ask you to explain the four laws of thermodynamics again?"

He joins in laughing with Teresa at the memory.

"She asked me about the helicopter that got us out that day," Lance says. "Why it didn't crash."

"Really?"

"Yeah, really. It's like bees...for a long time, scientists couldn't figure out how the little buggers fly. Sandy picked up on the same thing for helicopters...how they can fly."

Teresa nuzzles him again. "Just be thankful that one could fly that day."

Lance is drifting off, comfortable with the sensation of Teresa in his arms, in knowing Sam is safe, Sandy is safe, remembering that last grim day in Tunisia...

He remembers running back in the heat, holding Sandy close to his chest, Karim shouting into his cell phone, now back at the dig site, more shouts and yells, and the men guarding them, they...

They toss their AK-47s to the ground, start running away, going to the two sole pickup trucks, starting them up and driving away, tails of dust marking their retreat. Lance is dumbfounded. The trucks belong to Stanford. They've just been stolen!

Karim is still yelling into his cell phone, his free arm up in the air, like this movement can strengthen the cell phone signal, can signal his message.

Teresa takes Sandy from his arms just outside of the tents and says, "Where did you find her? Is she okay?"

Lance's chest is tight and it's hard to catch his breath. "Sandy...she's fine. We...found her...in a cave, just over those hills."

Teresa grabs Sandy and checks her over, and yells, "Sam! Over here! Right now!"

Lance whirls around. One by one the men who had worked with them are running away as well, dropping their hand tools, their shovels. Only Karim is still here, still shouting.

"Lance!" Teresa says, frantic. "What's wrong? Where is everyone?"

Lance pulls Sam to his side, and he says, "Sandy.... she found a cave. Full of guns, bombs, rockets. It's an arms cache...probably belonging to terrorists..."

Teresa looks wildly around their now deserted dig site. "Lance...what do we do? Where do we go?"

Even in this hot Tunisian sun, Lance feels frozen in place. He has always depended on the generosity and friendship of the locals whom he and the university have hired, and he has always convinced himself that he could bring his family here and work in a bubble of safety and protection.

What a fool he's been.

"Karim," he shouts. "Karim, what's going on?"

Karim turns away, still yelling, and Lance feels alone, abandoned, even with his family nearby.

And he wonders…who the hell is Karim talking to? Is he actually looking for help? Or something else? Is Karim upset, insulted over the pay dispute?

"Look!" Teresa screams.

She's pointing up at the hillside, where two and then three black-clad men appear, carrying AK-47s.

The stuttering gunfire stuns Lance, and he pulls his family down, turning over one of the tables piled high with recently excavated precious artifacts, hearing them smash and crash to the ground and not caring one bit.

Sandy and Sam are huddled under Teresa's arms, and Lance has a flash of memory, of learning how the Romans had sacked Carthage and its surrounding lands back in 146 BC and how women and children were put to the sword and slaughtered.

More men are up on the hillside, and some are running toward them.

"Lance!" Teresa yells. "We have to do something!"

Never in his life has he felt this helpless, and he starts to debate with himself: Should he send his family running while he and

Karim give themselves up, or should he and Karim try to get the weapons abandoned by their supposed guards and put up a desperate fight, or—

Karim yells in triumph. "See! See!"

Lance turns and looks to the east. Two helicopters are descending on the dig site, low and fast. Both are painted the same, with contrasting brown-and-tan schemes, but one looks to be a transport helicopter, and the other—

The other approaches the hill, starts firing its machine guns. Teresa screams, and Sam and Sandy hold their little hands against their ears. The transport helicopter swoops down beyond the tents, tearing one up with its rotor wash, throwing up clouds of dust and dirt, and Karim says, "Go, we go!"

Lance pushes, pulls, and drags Teresa and Sam and Sandy along, not caring about the artifacts, the records, their belongings, knowing only that the rattling machine with the spinning blades ahead of them is their lifeboat, their rescue.

Two soldiers with big helmets lean out of the side door, frantically waving their hands. Karim jumps in first, turns, and helps Sam and Sandy board, and as Lance is dragged in, there's a change in the pitch of the engine, and the helicopter lifts off.

Teresa is hugging him, crying, and she shouts. "Thank God we're safe! We're safe!"

Lance rolls over, and through the dust and dirt, he sees their dig site, sees two pickup trucks approaching, big black flags flapping at the rear...

And then he's awake in the uncomfortable bed in Levittown, thinking now what he thought back there, in that Tunisian Air Force helicopter, as they left that arms cache and their dig site behind.

They'll never be safe, ever again.

CHAPTER 31

AT 9:03 A.M. the next day, Gray Evans is back at the third-floor offices of his information contact, Abraham, sitting in one of the comfortable chairs around the conference table and reflecting on what he saw walking up to this building.

Which was nothing. His two parking attendants from the other day were gone.

What a city, what a world. Maybe his little interaction had put the two of them on the road to a fruitful life, but Gray wouldn't bet on it.

Hand clasping his cane tight, Abraham sits across from him and says, "Well, sometimes it comes down to skill, and sometimes it's luck. Last night it was luck."

"Glad that Lady Luck is smiling on you," Gray says, sipping on a cup of coffee Abraham has provided. "Did she flash her boobies at you, too?"

"Better than that," Abraham says with a smile. "Once I got started, I set up a nice little sniffing program that goes through every crack and crevice of the internet, looking for the family and where they might be. Relatives, places of employment, friends, former friends…a nice program that I devised myself, and then…well, it's like making this huge extravagant dinner from scratch and having everyone compliment you later on the Sara Lee cake you bought for dessert."

"Tasty," Glen says. "Go on."

Abraham smiles. "It was the boy, the ten-year-old kid. He popped up online last night for exactly twelve minutes, checking his Gmail account, before he logged off." Abraham shakes his head. "Kids nowadays, they don't know it, but they're living in a science fiction world. Most of them carry around a device that can access the complete stored knowledge of the human race, and they use it to send fart and booger jokes to each other."

Gray is getting impatient. "Yeah, kids nowadays…so where is the little punk?"

Abraham slides over a sheet of paper. "Here are the particulars. The ISP the kid was using came back to a David and Susan Barne of Levittown…but I don't think that's where the Sanderson family is staying."

"Why not?"

"Two reasons. Because the Barnes have no connection whatsoever to the Sandersons, and because the house right next door is owned by something called the Hampton Realty Trust."

"Which is what?"

Gray sees that Abraham once again has the happy and serene smile of a man who knows it all and who loves rubbing that in someone else's face. Gray allows him that little victory, because it'll be the last smile he ever flashes.

"Because Hampton Realty Trust is a front organization," Abraham says. "There's a shell corporation behind that, and another one behind that…all very hush-hush and well concealed…except to me. The home's real owners reside in Langley, Virginia."

"The CIA," Gray says.

"Bingo," Abraham says. One hand still grasping his cane, Abraham reaches over and taps a line on the sheet of paper. "And check this little bit of information out. The wife and mother, Teresa Sanderson, she has a family connection with law enforcement. You might want to keep that in mind before you proceed."

Gray looks again at the information Abraham has provided, nods his head, and folds the sheet of paper and places it in his coat pocket.

"Great work, Abraham," he says. "The very best. Which is why this is going to pain me so much."

And he pulls out his 9mm Smith & Wesson pistol.

CHAPTER 32

LEONARD BROOKS IS dreaming about his response to his first fatal motor vehicle accident as a New York State Trooper—a stolen Toyota Camry had struck a bridge abutment on the Thruway outside of Buffalo and had ejected two high school boys through the windshield—when his bedroom phone rings.

He wakes up, glad for the interruption. The dream was going into some strange, dark places, which Leonard assumed was a side effect of the stress he's been under while trying to locate his cousin. The dream had started with the actual memory—the local fire department pumper truck had eventually come by to wash down the blood and brain matter from the abutment's concrete—but then it had taken a dark turn: Leonard had found himself standing in a drainage ditch, the bloody water swirling around his ankles.

He grabs the phone and murmurs a greeting.

A very chipper and alert Beth Draper is on the other end. "Gosh, aren't we the Gloomy Gus this morning."

"Just got off shift," he says, rubbing at his eyes. He hates the night shifts the most, for a variety of reasons. The main one is his neighbors, obsessed landscapers who are always outside after the sun rises with their leaf blowers and lawn mowers.

But so far, it's been quiet, except for this phone call. He rubs at his grainy eyes again and says, "What do you have?"

"What makes you think I have anything?" Beth asks. "Maybe I'm calling you because I'm going to be in your neck of the woods and I want to offer you the chance to wine, dine, and bed me…and not necessarily in that order."

"Beth…"

She laughs. "All right, couldn't help myself." And then the tone of her voice changes to the experienced intelligence official she is. "Your cousin, she has a son, right?"

"Yeah," Leonard says. "Samuel. Eight or nine. Too smart for his own good."

"Well, the lad is ten, and last night he was online for a few minutes, checking his Gmail account."

Leonard is now wide awake. He swings his legs around and sits up, and fumbles on the nightstand for a pen and a scrap of paper.

"Go on," he says.

"Your smart young fella accessed a computer belonging to a David and Susan Barne of Levittown."

"Perfect," he says, now with pen in hand. "Where is it?"

She gives him an address, which he scribbles down, and she says, "Before you race over, hotshot, here's the deal. I don't think he's there."

"What?"

"Hold on, hold on," she says. "It's like this. I didn't see any blatant connection between your cousin and the Barne family, and I did a little digging, and found out that the neighboring house belongs to a realty company…which has some spooky connections."

"How spooky?"

"I can't tell, not right now," Beth admits. "It's pretty well protected, but it's government-connected, that's for sure, and I don't mean the embarrassing government we have up in Albany."

"The feds."

"Yeah." Beth gives him that address, and he scribbles that down as well, and she says, "My guess is that the place is a safe house of some kind. You still sure your cousin and her hubby don't have enemies?"

"Positive," Leonard says. "She writes books, he digs in the dirt. How can you get enemies from that?"

Beth says, "You'd be surprised, my friend. In today's world, it's very easy to get on someone's enemy's list."

Despite the growing anticipation that he now knows where his cousin is located, he yawns and says, "Excuse me for that, okay."

"Sure."

There's a noise outside, like someone's knocking at the door. He says, "All right, safe house. Got it. You've done good, Beth."

"Of course I have," she says. "But a safe house…it's only safe depending who's there, and who might be out there looking to do them harm. I found out where they live. That doesn't mean that bad guys won't do the same. And soon."

CHAPTER 33

GRAY EVANS IS stunned when Abraham suddenly laughs at the barrel of the pistol he is pointing at the man's heart.

Abraham says, "For real? You threaten me with that gun after all the times you've hired me?"

Gray supposes he should shoot and get it over with, but something is going on with Abraham and he wants to know more.

Gray says, "Nothing personal. After a while you need to clean up your business dealings, your patterns, and start new somewhere else. Otherwise you leave behind a traceable trail."

Abraham shakes his head. "You think I've survived all this time without taking precautions?"

His info man now really has his attention.

"Precautions," Gray says. "Go on."

Abraham holds up his cane. "See how tight I always hold this? It's a dead man's switch. You do me harm or kill me, and I drop the cane. And when I do that, this entire floor goes up in one hell of a bang."

Gray stares at Abraham, who doesn't flinch, doesn't move. Abraham adds, "Based on this neighborhood, that might even jump-start a revamp of the entire block, which means a lot of these people won't be able to afford their housing. You really want to do that, Gray?"

Gray laughs, puts his pistol away. "Only joking. That's all."

"Sure," Abraham says. "And your sense of humor just doubled your invoice."

CHAPTER 34

THE INTELLIGENCE OFFICER known as the Big Man moves as fast as his bulk allows him down the corridor leading to his office, because the morning news of the latest terrorist attack in the London subway has forced him into work two hours ahead of schedule.

Just outside his office, an IT worker—and who cares what her name is—is standing there in response to the call he had made downstairs. The Big Man passes over his handheld device and says, "It crapped out on me last night. Get me a new one, transfer the information, and let me know immediately if there were any calls I missed."

"Very good, sir," she says, and she moves quickly past him as he unlocks his door and goes inside.

Not much time and a lot of work to do, and the only thing he does is to grab a fresh legal pad. He leaves, heading to an urgent staff meeting to deal with what's going on in London.

He locks his office door behind him and is about six feet down the hallway when he thinks he hears his office phone ringing.

Should he go back?

No, he thinks.
It can wait.
It has to wait.
London is burning.
He keeps moving.

CHAPTER 35

IN A NEW rental vehicle, Gray Evans slowly drives along a quiet street in Levittown. By God, there it is, the little house that holds his target.

Quiet, with a fence out at the rear and no easy means of escape.

Right in front of him.

The trunk of his rental car has enough firepower to outfit a Georgia county sheriff's department, and he's tempted—oh, is he tempted—to park the car, pop open the trunk, and go in: a blitz attack.

No delay, no waiting around, just go right in and start blasting.

Very tempting.

He slows down…it's a small house, one-story, and, based on what he knows about Levittown, it's probable this house doesn't have a basement or an attic.

Could be pretty easy.

Could be.

He speeds up.

He hasn't stayed alive this long by relying on "could be."

*   *   *

An hour later he leaves the town offices of Hempstead, New York, which govern the hamlet of Levittown. He's spent some time with the easygoing and friendly town officials, who have passed on the tax records for the property where the Sandersons are living.

The best part of this research is that the tax records present the house as a typical one-story Cape Cod, with no basement and no attic. It has only seven rooms: three bedrooms, two bathrooms, kitchen, and living room

Thanks to these very courteous small-town officials, he now has a detailed floor plan of how best to kill the person he needs to kill.

Still...even with all this information, he needs to tilt the playing field more in his favor.

How best to get in and do his job?

He has an idea. He checks his watch, thinks he needs to call a new intel source—though Abraham is breathing, he might as well be dead to him—to confirm the information on Teresa's law enforcement connection.

If all goes well, within the hour, his target—and, if need be, the entire Sanderson family—will be dead.

CHAPTER 36

THE BIG MAN unlocks the door to his office and walks in. He's exhausted, thirsty, and hungry, and the day ahead of him stretches like one long session on a chain gang. He's unable to move, unable to do anything besides react to what's going on across the Atlantic.

"Sir?" A tapping noise at the side of his open door. The IT tech from the morning comes in and says, "Here's your new phone, sir. All information, passwords, connections, and files successfully transferred."

He holds his thick hand out, gives her a quick "thank you"—even if he doesn't know her name, there's no need to be rude—and she leaves as he powers up the phone. He starts sliding through the screens, checking and seeing—

What the hell?

Pressing the phone against his ear, he listens to the message again and drops his new piece of equipment on his desk. Then he picks up his secure interior line and dials four digits. When the man on the other line picks up he says, "Did I or did I not receive a notification from a James Williams, from Department G-17, last night?"

"Ah, sir, it appears—"

"There was no follow-up!" the Big Man yells. "None!"

"Ah—"

"Why wasn't I promptly informed?"

"Sir, a call was made to your office this morning and—"

"That's not confirmation!" he yells. "You and your section have just killed four innocents…" My God, what a screw-up! He goes on, "And by the end of the day, you and Williams will be in custody, pending an internal review."

The Big Man slams the phone down, takes a breath, picks it up again, and dials another number.

"Domestic Operations." A female voice.

He checks the nearest clock for the time. Do they have enough of it?

"We have an emerging situation in Levittown, New York," he says, checking a file and then rapidly giving the woman the address. "I need a response team."

"When?"

He takes another breath, knowing this isn't going to end well.

"As of last night," he finally says.

CHAPTER 37

LANCE HASN'T SLEPT well. After a quiet and strained breakfast, it seems like everyone in the household is off in their own little world. Lance helps Teresa with the dishes and checks in on Sam, who's back at work at the small desk, putting together his dinosaur model, hunched over in concentration, looking like one of those old medieval engravings of a monk working on an illuminated manuscript.

Lance asks, "How's it going?"

Sam says, "About halfway done."

His boy doesn't lift his head, and Lance is sure the kiddo is still ashamed over last night's events, and so he leaves him alone and checks on Sam's sister.

Sandy is on her immaculately made bed and he says, "How are you doing, honey?"

She turns a page, and he recognizes the book he had given her about Hannibal. "I'll be finishing this book at about 2:00 p.m. today, Dad." Another page flip. "And there are no other books to read."

"I'm sure I can find one."

"No, you're wrong," she says crisply. "I've checked every room in the house, the bags, and the shelves. This is the last book."

"Then we'll have to get you a new one," he says.

"Good," she says. "I've talked to Jason. You need to talk to him. He says we can only go shopping for new books if all of us go together. So we need to go together, but we can't, because you told Sam he had to stay in his room."

Lance says, "We'll take care of it, sweetheart."

"Good," Sandy says, and for a moment, Lance has the ugly thought that his young daughter has just dismissed him. *She doesn't mean it*, he tells himself.

He goes to the kitchen for a post-breakfast cup of coffee and surprises Teresa, who seems to have been looking through some of her photographs from Tunisia. He hasn't yet seen the one that's up on her computer. It seems to have been taken in a marketplace somewhere back there.

Teresa jumps and closes the photo program. Quickly she says, "How are the super kids?"

"One's being quiet for a nice change, the other one's concerned she's about to run out of books."

Teresa says nothing, goes back to her laptop. When he's finished with his coffee, he steals another glance at her laptop.

No photo program.

No Word document.

Nothing to do with her book.

His wife is quietly playing solitaire, like she's…

Killing time.

Jason is at the rear door where he dragged Sam in last night, looking out at the backyard. There's shrubbery and an old wooden fence. Shouts and cries can be heard from young children playing on the other side of the fence, and Jason's head moves with every sound.

To be this alert all the time…Lance is impressed by the skill, the dedication, the strength this man has.

"Can I get you something, Jason? Cup of coffee? Orange juice?"

"No, sir, I'm fine."

"Glad to hear it," Lance says. He stands there uncomfortably, like he's been called to the principal's office, and he says, "You know…when we got here, we were told it'd be less than a week before we'd leave."

"That's right, sir."

Lance says, "So we might leave today."

"You might."

"Then…I want to thank you for everything. I…we'll never forget what you've done for us."

Jason slowly turns and says, "I haven't done a damn thing for you."

The man's face is troubled, like he's under some extra, awful burden. Like he's got more on his shoulders than just the job of protecting the four of them.

Jason clears his throat. "I need to tell you something. I shouldn't…but I will."

The sound of the doorbell ringing startles Lance, making him spill some hot coffee on his hand.

Jason brushes by him. "Lockdown. Now."

CHAPTER 38

JASON IS PLEASANTLY surprised at how quickly the Sanderson family moves under his direction. No fuss, no raised voices, moving like boots nearing the end of basic training. In the tiny bathroom he scoops up Sandy—"You be a good girl, all right?"—and puts her in the bathtub, and Sam jumps right in without being asked. He moves the kids around so Sandy is lying down, with her brother nestled on top.

Sam looks up, eyes wide with fear. "I…"

"Quiet," Jason says. "Protect your older sister, okay?"

Sam nods silently. The last he sees of the boy is when he picks up the heavy Kevlar blanket to drape it over his cuddled form.

The mother and father are seated on the floor, legs pulled up so he can walk by. Considerate. As he moves past them, something odd happens.

Teresa, the wife, holds her hand up.

What?

It comes to him what she's looking for, and he gives the hand a quick squeeze and steps out in the hallway, closing the bathroom door behind him. There's a little *click* as it's locked.

Good. First time they had done this, as a drill, the father had forgotten to lock the door.

Nice to see everyone doing well today.

The doorbell rings again and Jason quickly moves to the front door, gives a quick look through a side window, sees it's a cop standing there.

Cops again, he thinks. He wishes there were that many cops in his neighborhood when he was growing up in Seattle.

He opens the door, sees the man's wearing a New York State Trooper uniform, and immediately knows why the guy is here: Teresa has a relative in the force.

"Yes?" he asks. "Can I help you?"

The trooper, in his immaculate gray uniform, campaign hat, bright purple necktie, and shiny badge pinned to his shirt, looks friendly and apologetic. "This is going to sound strange, but could you bear with me for a moment, sir? I'm looking for my cousin, Teresa Sanderson, and her family."

Jason is running through what to say to this friendly young man before shooing him away, when the phone belted to his side starts to screech at him.

He glances down for a second.

It's a second long enough.

The trooper has a pistol in his hands and with two loud, bright hammer blows, Jason is shot twice in the chest.

CHAPTER 39

LANCE HAS HIS arm around Teresa. The sound of the two gunshots seems to echo in the tiny bathroom, and Teresa screams, and from the bathtub, Sam starts yelling—his voice muffled by the Kevlar—"It's my fault, it's my fault, I used the computer, it's my fault!"

He starts crying and Sandy shrieks, and Lance goes over to the bathtub, lifts the Kevlar blanket, looks at the scared faces of his children, "It's okay, it's okay, you just stay there, okay?"

Lance drops the blanket, sees that Teresa's face is pale with shock, her hands tightly clasped, and says, "What about—"

Suddenly, he shuts up. Neither one of them has a cell phone, because both were confiscated two weeks ago when Teresa was in the middle of calling her mother.

He looks to Teresa, then looks up at the tiny window over the toilet.

Trapped.

There's a knock at the door.

Teresa yelps and crawls over to him, curled next to him by the bathtub. Their son and daughter are wailing from underneath the protective blanket.

"Guys?" A new voice from outside. "There's been an incident.

It's safe now. Come on out. I'm a state trooper, just like Leonard. More police will be here any minute."

Teresa grabs Lance's upper arm, whispers, "That's not the phrase to get us to open the door…what does it mean?"

Lance says, "It means Jason's dead."

CHAPTER 40

AFTER HE GETS no response from the family locked inside the bathroom, Gray Evans tries the handle once again.

Still locked.

Okay, not a problem.

So far, the procedure's going fine, and Gray sees no reason why it shouldn't keep on going so. Hell, even an hour ago, his second intel choice, Neil, was quick and efficient over the phone, getting him the name and address of a local off-duty state trooper. Gray had killed the man with a quick bullet to the head and haphazardly gotten dressed in his uniform, clipping its accessories in their most likely places.

And now it was simple—the entire family in one room.

Gray stands back, takes position, starts to aim his pistol at the doorknob, and then it begins to turn.

"Okay, we're coming out." A shaky male voice comes from inside.

Perfect. How sweetly perfect.

The door opens a crack just as Gray hears the creak and scrape of a window opening…

The door opens a little more. A woman is standing on the toilet, shoving a small figure through the tiny window, its legs going through—

"Hey!" he yells, bringing up his pistol, wondering where the father is, and—

A man comes from behind the door.

With something in his hand.

Gray turns and

Yells as the man sprays him in the face and eyes with something harsh and burning.

CHAPTER 41

RONALD TEMPLE IS lightly dozing in his Barcalounger when the sound of two gunshots wakes him up. His consciousness goes from zero to sixty in one second. He's served on the job with officers who freaked out when they heard a truck backfire or a manhole cover slam shut, but Ronald has always known better: someone has just fired two shots next door.

He scrambles up in the chair, blanket sliding off, .38 revolver in his lap, as he shakily picks up the phone, dials 911.

When the male operator answers and goes through the usual bored answering shtick—"911, what is the nature and location of your emergency?"—Ronald carefully says, "Shots fired," rattles off the address next door, and drops the phone.

He doesn't have time to answer questions or fill out the operator's checklist, so he grabs the revolver and heaves himself off the chair.

Thank God Helen is out shopping. He doesn't want her here, where she'd be both in danger and telling him not to do what he's about to do.

Ronald tears the oxygen hose away and makes his way to the entryway with his lungs burning.

His hands are shaking.

Damn it, like a rookie alone on his first night shift!

He puts the revolver down, goes to the portable oxygen tank, cranks it up, drapes the tubes around his head, and opens the door.

Picks up the revolver.

This time he won't screw up.

This time he won't be hiding home, drunk.

Ronald goes to the house, revolver still shaking in one hand, his other hand dragging his green oxygen tank behind him.

This time he will do what has to be done.

CHAPTER 42

EYES BURNING–BRINGING back a memory of being exposed to tear gas during basic training—Gray swears, stumbles back, and fires off two shots at the door as it slams in front of him.

Damn it!

He wipes at his eyes, swearing again. Whatever the son of a bitch sprayed at him is burning and clouding up his eyes. He can feel them swelling.

Time to move.

He moves away from the bathroom, going through the kitchen and living room, bouncing off a chair, until he ends up at the front door. The big guy he had shot earlier is still on the floor, and Gray wants to make sure his rear is secure, so he fires another shot at the guy's head before springing out the door.

Gray is out the door and—

Thump!

Can you believe the luck?

He's bumped into the two kids, who have fallen to the lawn, crying.

But his eyes are burning and he can't tell which is which.

No matter.

He grabs one and then the other, starts running a hand over their heads and—

"Stop right there!" a man shouts.

CHAPTER 43

RONALD TEMPLE IS on the lawn of his odd neighbors, revolver in both of his shaking hands, aiming it straight at the man standing in front of him, who looks nice and sharp in a New York State Trooper's uniform. The officer has his arms around the young boy and girl who live here. Ronald's lungs are burning and his legs are so weak he feels like his knees are about to give way.

But he stands his ground.

There have been three more gunshots since the first two woke him up, and he won't back away.

"Who are you?" he demands, straining to make his voice sound strong.

This is all wrong. His earlier plan was to attack his neighbors if they turned out to be terrorists, but what's with the gunshots and this guy standing in front of him?

The man—whose eyes are red and swollen—curses and says, "Who the hell do you think I am? Put that gun away!"

"Not until I know what's going on," Ronald says. The boy is crying, snot dribbling from his nose. The young girl is…just staring, face frozen.

"What's going on? I'm a damn state trooper, and I'm ordering you to put that gun away. There's backup coming."

Ronald swallows, his throat sand-dry. "Let the kids go. Or else."

"Or else what?"

"You know what else," Ronald says, again hating how weak his voice is.

"Yeah?" the man says, not moving at all, the kids still in his grasp. "Sorry, old man, I don't think you're going to do a damn thing."

CHAPTER 44

JASON TYLER REGAINS consciousness.

His right ear is ringing like a bell.

His lower chest and belly...feel cold, numb—like he's been hit twice by a sledgehammer.

You've been shot.

Twice.

Because you screwed up.

A memory surfaces from when he was a kid, watching some nature documentary that showed a rattlesnake attack. It attacked so fast, the human eye couldn't see it...and the camera had to slow down to show the coiled rattlesnake extend in one long, looping motion, mouth open, fangs displayed.

That trooper.

One hell of a rattlesnake.

Okay.

Situation...

We are seriously screwed.

Jason knows from experience that he has just a few minutes before the shock wears off and the real pain kicks in, so it's time to get to work.

He reaches down to his side, retrieves his government-issued phone. There's a side switch that he presses...but he misses it. He tries twice more and then...

Success.

All right, then.

Panic button pressed.

Meaning the cavalry— well armed and well equipped—should be here in a few minutes.

But...

Jason rolls over so he's on his hands and knees.

Look at all the damn blood.

He groans and stands up.

The mission...

Have to do the mission.

The cavalry is on its way, but it'll get here way too late.

He weaves, finds his weapon under his shirt.

Get to work.

I have to protect...

Have to do the job.

Jason weaves again, going to the door.

It seems like it's a mile away.

CHAPTER 45

GRAY WIPES AT his eyes. His full vision is almost back.

He stares in disbelief at the old man standing in front of him, skinny as a cornstalk, wearing baggy slacks and a flannel shirt, damn oxygen tank at his side, tubes running out of his big nose, pointing a revolver at him.

"Drop your weapon!" he yells. "I'm a state trooper! Drop it!"

The old man coughs and says, "No…no, you're not!"

The kids are squirming under his grasp and Gray says, "What do you mean I'm not a trooper, you sonavabitch?"

The old man pulls the hammer back on the revolver, cocking it.

"You have a badge on your uniform shirt," he says, now gasping, like his lungs are collapsing. "New York State Troopers don't wear badges on their shirts."

With his moving hands, Gray finds the long hair of the girl.

Finally!

He pushes the boy away, removes his weapon, and starts to pull the trigger, holding the girl in place with his other hand.

CHAPTER 46

RONALD HAD SEEN many amazing things while on the job and working security, but he can't believe how fast the fake trooper moves when he pushes the boy away, swivels the girl around, brings up his pistol, pushes the muzzle against the back of the girl's head.

Pulling the trigger on his .38 revolver is a heavy tug for Ronald, and, God, he's not quick enough, he won't make it, he's going to fail again and—

A gunshot erupts, loud and hammering.

He gasps, stumbling back.

The fake trooper grunts, sways, and the little girl breaks away from his grasp.

Ronald starts to squeeze the trigger again but the man before him slowly turns and collapses on the lawn.

God…

From inside the house comes the big guy—the bodyguard, the one he thought was a terrorist cell leader—staggering, an arm tight around his bloody belly, the other hand holding a pistol.

Ronald goes to him, dragging the oxygen tank behind him, clattering. The young boy and girl are standing by the front of the house.

The wounded man comes closer.

He sees Ronald standing there.

Ronald says, "Hold on…the police are coming. They'll be here any second."

The man stops, weaves.

He opens his mouth and blood trickles out.

Ronald says, "Hold on, don't say anything, you should just sit down…"

The man spits out the blood. "The girl…the young girl…is she safe?"

Ronald can't believe the question. All that's going on and he asks about the girl?

"Answer me!" the man says, voice stronger. "The girl…is she safe?"

Ronald checks her one more time, standing there with her brother, arms around each other.

"Yes," Ronald says. "She's safe. She's fine."

"Thanks," he says. Then he smiles and collapses to the ground.

CHAPTER 47

AFTER SHE HEARS more gunshots, Teresa pushes her husband aside and lurches to the front door.

Oh, God, look at that blood on the floor.

Lance is saying something about staying here and staying safe, and Teresa refuses to listen to a single word.

Her children are out there.

And she won't stay inside.

If there are men out there waiting to kill her because of the photos she took back at that Tunisian marketplace, well, she will die protecting her children and take her punishment.

She unlocks the door, pulls it open, and races out. Outside into the fresh air and sunlight and grass and with Lance right at her heels—

There they are—Sandy and Sam!

She gathers them in her arms, squeezes them, squeezes them, squeezes them, and says, "Oh, my babies, are you all right? Are you all right?"

Sam is sobbing but Sandy says, "We're not hurt, Mom, but please..."

"What?"

"Stop squeezing me so hard. It's hurting."

Teresa bursts out in a sob and turns around, hearing sirens in the distance. A man in a state trooper's uniform is on his back, mouth open, not moving. Lance goes to him, kicks a nearby pistol away across the lawn. Their nosy neighbor is standing there, shocked, a revolver in a shaking hand, oxygen tank by his side, tubes running from his nose.

He tries to say something, but he coughs and coughs and nearly doubles over from the hacking.

From inside her family's embrace, Teresa turns to the man and says, "What is it?"

"That man," the older man says. "He…he died saving your daughter."

Teresa sobs, turning her head away from the two dead men on the lawn. A helicopter flies overhead, the sirens are louder, and Teresa says, "Lance…it makes sense. God, now it makes sense."

Lance says, "What in hell makes sense in all of this?"

"You know how I said Jason looked guilty all the time?" Teresa asks. "And you said I was making things up?"

"I remember," Lance says. "And I'm sorry I said that…I was beginning to see it, too. There was something going on with him."

Cruisers roar down the road, screech to a halt. Another helicopter swoops overhead. Teresa squeezes her children tight again. She refuses to let go of them.

"He was guilty all right," Teresa says, feeling tears roll down her cheeks. "Guilty because his job wasn't to protect us. It was to protect Sandy, first and foremost. You saw how he always put Sandy first in the bathtub, covering her with her brother? How he always was closest to her? How Sandy was first in the Yukon, last one out? That's why…"

Lance is stunned.

Teresa…she's right.

He looks to his special daughter, who's calmly looking out at the chaos of police cars, ambulances, and other vehicles quickly filling up the road.

Their Sandy…. He is so proud of who she is, so scared of what awaits her.

CHAPTER 48

LEONARD BROOKS IS violating about a half-dozen procedures and protocols, racing toward the address in Levittown where his cousin and her family are located, but he doesn't care.

The sirens are wailing, the lights are flashing, and with every twist and turn in this crowded suburb, he nearly scrapes or rams into a parked car. The radio traffic is one long, anguished chatter: an off-duty trooper has been shot in his home…shots fired at a Levittown residence…possible state trooper down…more shots…officer needs assistance, officer needs assistance…

The tires screech in protest as he slides through another curve, and up ahead…

There.

A confused scrum of police vehicles from what looks to be about a half-dozen jurisdictions are parked in a jagged mess up ahead. He pulls over, grabs his campaign hat, bails out of the cruiser, and starts running.

Civilians are standing on their little front lawns, peering at all the activity, tossing questions at him as he goes by.

"What's going on?"

"Who got shot?"

"Is this an act of terrorism?"

A police line with yellow tape has been set up, and he is waved through as he ducks under and gets closer, just in time to see Teresa, her husband, Lance, and the two kids—Sam and Sandy—being escorted into an armored SUV. Serious-looking men and women in full SWAT battle-rattle surround them.

"Hey, Teresa!" Leonard yells, and, by God, with all the confusion, sirens sounding, and steady roar of helicopters overhead, she hears him.

She turns and waves with a free hand, and he waves back, and then that's it.

The family is shoved into the SUV. It backs out of the driveway, escorted by three cruisers, and roars away from the crime scene.

And what a crime scene. Two bodies are on the grass, covered in yellow cloth. Forensics markers are being set up, and measurements and photographs are being taken. There are lots of men and women in civvies, with weapons and handheld radios in their hands, definitely not looking like civilians right now.

A SWAT team guy has his helmet off, and his close-cropped white hair is smeared with sweat. He's carrying an M4 rifle as he strolls over.

"Hey," he says.

"How's it going," Leonard says, taking in the scene. There's an old man with an oxygen tank, sitting in a folding lawn chair, gesturing to the house as two women stand next to him, taking notes.

"About as close a run-in as I've ever seen," the SWAT officer says. "That one"—and he points to the ground—"is dressed up in a trooper's uniform, exactly like yours."

"He's not a trooper," Leonard says. "One of my guys—not in my troop—got shot an hour ago, and his uniform was stolen."

"Jesus," the SWAT man says. "Well, the other one"—he points to the second shape— "was some sort of bodyguard for this family. Then the goddamn O.K. Corral broke out here about a half hour ago, gunfire left and right, if you can believe it in this little town."

"I can believe it," Leonard says. "The family?"

The SWAT man hesitates. "I saw you call out to the mom. You know her?"

"She's my cousin."

"No shit…well, so you know, they're all safe."

Leonard looks around at the vehicles, the armed men, the two helicopters hovering overhead.

"Yes," he says. "But for how long?"

CHAPTER 49

THE BIG MAN is in his office, watching the continuing coverage of that morning's terrorist attack in London, when the Thin Woman comes in without knocking.

She stands in front of his desk and says, "Under control, but by the thinnest of margins. Cover story will be a drug deal gone bad, something like that, with a heroic state police trooper killed in battle. We might have to give their neighbor—a retired NYPD cop—a clandestine medal to keep his mouth shut about what happened in his neighborhood. I think he'll be happy with that."

The Big Man says, "Wasn't the murdered state trooper at home on his day off?"

"He died for his state and country," the Thin Woman says. "What else do people need to know? How do we stand on Clarkson?"

The Big Man says, "She's on her way back to the states, should be landing at Andrews in about six hours. Then the real work will begin."

The Thin Woman shakes her head. "Hard to believe we've been waiting so long for her."

"We needed an ISIS expert, a cryptography expert, and someone who knows how to work with a child with Asperger's who's memorized reams of encrypted intelligence documents," he points out. "We got Clarkson. Be thankful we do, and that the little girl is still alive."

"What about the Sanderson family, then?" the Thin Woman asks.

"When the job is done, they'll be given compensation, new IDs, and a new life somewhere."

The Thin Woman pauses before turning to leave. "They didn't volunteer for this."

The Big Man gestures up to a television screen, showing smoke billowing out of a Tube station in London. "Who does?"

CHAPTER 50

THREE MONTHS AFTER leaving Levittown, Lance Sanderson returns to his family's new home, a little beach house on a remote stretch of Florida's Gulf Coast. He parks the old Chevy pickup in the crushed-shell driveway—imagine him, driving a pickup truck!—and grabs a small leather bag before going around back.

It's a gorgeous day on the Gulf, with sailboats and fishing boats out there, people playing and working, and birds weaving overhead. At least one of those birds is man-made, because one of the promises given when they moved here was that they would be watched, 24/7, by an unmanned drone.

Lance walks out back and his safe family is sitting underneath a striped awning over the rear deck. Since they're near the beach now, Sam is fascinated with seashells, and he's sitting in just a bathing suit, examining his latest haul at a round glass-covered table. One of the first days they had been here, Sam had shown him a bit of metal and plastic and had asked, "Dad, what's this? Is it important?" And Lance had laughed and passed it back. "An old transistor, from an old radio. Not important at all."

But for some reason that hadn't disappointed Sam…in fact, it had seemed to cheer him up.

Sam's sister is also dressed in her bathing suit, and since she's near the ocean, now she's fascinated with navies and warships. She's been working her way through the fifteen-volume *History of United States Naval Operations in World War II,* written by the historian Samuel Eliot Morison.

Both of his kids ignore him as he walks onto the deck. Typical…and considering what they've all been through, it feels so good that it nearly brings him to tears.

Teresa is working on her laptop, wearing a one-piece black bathing suit and a wide straw hat. Lance gives her a kiss as he sits down next to her. Teresa's lips taste of salt water and tanning lotion, and Lance hopes he might have some time with his love this afternoon while the kids are otherwise engaged.

Teresa says, "How were things at the range?"

"Getting better," he says, putting the leather bag with his licensed Glock pistol on the deck. Even with their movements tracked by a drone, he will never, ever solely depend on anyone else to protect his family. "I managed to get more and more of my shots dead center. How are the kids?"

She says, "Kids are fine."

"And you?"

"You know, I'm beginning to like writing children's books, even if it is under a pen name," Teresa says. "You can make things up, and you can't do that writing a guidebook."

Lance stretches his legs out. "Good. Looks like I'm traveling next week. Consulting gig at Air Force Special Operations up at Hurlburt. Telling them what I know about that stretch of Tunisia. And you…?"

Teresa smiles. "And what?"

"Don't be a tease," Lance says. "What did the doctor say?"

Teresa shifts in her chair, revealing a slight swell in her belly. "Three months along for sure, everything's healthy…and, hate to spoil the surprise, but the kids are getting a new brother."

Lances leans over, kisses and embraces his wife. Their son and daughter continue to ignore them. "You know what we're going to name him…"

"No debate here, lion," she says.

Lance gently strokes his wife's belly and whispers into it, "Little Jason, one of these days, we'll tell you about the hero you were named after…"

He chokes up. "Until then, you'll always be safe with us. Forever."

ABOUT THE AUTHORS

James Patterson has written more bestsellers and created more enduring fictional characters than any other novelist writing today. He lives in Florida with his family.

Brendan DuBois of New Hampshire is the award-winning author of twenty novels and more than 150 short stories, and his works have appeared in nearly a dozen countries. He is also a *Jeopardy!* game show champion.